## Seeing Amy with the horse told Ty exactly who she was.

Ty talked her through the sequence a few more times. Her face was absolutely glowing as she began to understand that the horse was responding to her slightest move.

"Everyone and everything is responding to us all the time at some level. Sometimes it's so subtle we don't know what we've told them."

*For instance, her kiss had told him she was hungry. But her eyes were saying she wasn't ready.*

"Okay, lower your hand and move your eyes to his shoulder."

The horse skidded to a halt. He turned in, his eyes riveted on her.

"Scratch his ears. And his forehead. Say something to him."

"Ben, I think I'm in love with you."

Her voice was husky and sweet, and it seemed to Ty a man could die to hear such words coming from her.

His next instructions, intended for the horse, were instructions he needed to heed himself.

"Now, turn and walk away."

Not that he could. Not while they were snowed in here together. But there were many ways to walk away.

And he should know, because he'd done most of them at one time or another.

"I don't want to walk away," she said, stroking Ben's nose with soft reverence. "I want to stay like this forever."

Yup, she was the kind of girl who could turn a man's thoughts to forever.

Dear Reader,

I hate to choose a favorite story, because it's something like choosing a favorite child. Having said that, the hero of this story grabbed me from the moment he sauntered into my imagination and leveled me a look from under the brim of his hat. I am totally in love with him. Ty Halliday is quiet, strong, sexy, calm *and* a cowboy. Can you imagine being snowed in with him?

That's exactly what happens to my heroine, Amy, a soft-hearted young widow disillusioned with love. Add to the mix the amazing ranch country of Southern Alberta, a baby and Christmas a-comin' and I think this becomes one of the most tender tales I've ever told!

I hope you enjoy it. If you do, would you come visit me on Facebook and let me know? I am amazed by how technology has given us this wonderful ability to connect.

Wishing you the most wonderful Christmas ever,

Cara

# CARA COLTER

*Snowed in at the Ranch*

HARLEQUIN®
entertain, enrich, inspire™

Recycling programs
for this product may
not exist in your area.

ISBN-13: 978-0-373-17846-9

SNOWED IN AT THE RANCH

First North American Publication 2012

www.Harlequin.com

**Printed in U.S.A.**

**Cara Colter** lives in British Columbia with her partner, Rob, and eleven horses. She has three grown children and a grandson. She is a recent recipient of an *RT Book Reviews* Career Achievement Award in the Love and Laughter category. Cara loves to hear from readers, and you can contact her or learn more about her through her website: www.cara-colter.com.

**Books by Cara Colter**

BATTLE FOR THE SOLDIER'S HEART
THE COP, THE PUPPY AND ME
TO DANCE WITH A PRINCE
RESCUED BY HIS CHRISTMAS ANGEL
WINNING A GROOM IN 10 DATES
RESCUED IN A WEDDING DRESS

**Other titles by this author available in ebook format.**

To my daughter, Cassidy:

*Love you forever.*

# CHAPTER ONE

Ty Halliday was beyond exhaustion. The driving mix of sleet and snow had soaked through his oilskin slicker hours ago. Icy water was sluicing off the back of his hat's brim, inside his upturned collar and straight down his spine.

The horse stumbled, as exhausted as his rider, dark setting in too fast.

But beneath all the discomfort, Ty allowed himself satisfaction. He'd found the entire herd. The three cows that shuffled along in front of him were the last of them.

It had been sixteen hours, roughly, since he'd found the broken fence, the cougar tracks. He counted himself lucky most of the herd had petered out and allowed themselves to be herded home, long before these three.

Tracks in fresh snow told the story of the herd splitting in a dozen different directions, the cougar locking in on these three, finally giving up and prowling away down Halliday Creek. These cows, in a panic, had kept on going, almost to the summer range, way up the mountain.

Below him, Ty could see the lights of his house winking against the growing darkness. It made him impatient for hot food, a stiff drink, a scalding shower and his bed.

But the horse, Ben, was young and had already demonstrated great heart, had given everything he had, and so Ty did not push him, but let the young gelding set his own pace down a trail that was slick with new snow.

Finally, finally, the cows were back with the herd, the pasture fences secured, Ben fed and watered. Ty followed a path from the barn, worn deep by a hundred years of Halliday boots, to where the "new" house sat on the top of a knoll of land, in the shadow of the mountain behind it.

The house was called new because it shared the property with the "old" homestead place, which his father had built for his first wife twenty-five years before Ty had been born.

Ty swayed on his back porch, his hand going to the doorknob.

Where it froze.

What had he heard?

Silence.

He cocked his head, listening hard, but heard only the lonely whistle of a December wind under the rafters of the house.

Ty felt he was suffering the delusions of a man who had pushed himself to his limit, and then a mile or two beyond it.

But he was frowning now, thinking of the lights inside his house that had winked him home. He lived alone. He was pretty damned sure that he had not left any lights on when he'd left way before dawn this morning.

The sound came again, and he took a startled step back, nearly tumbling down his back-porch steps.

The sound was definitely coming from *inside* his house. It was an almost shockingly happy sound. His tired mind grappled with it. He hadn't had a television for years. He didn't own a computer. Had he left the radio on?

No. He had not turned on anything this morning, some distress note in the faraway bawl of a cow letting him know something had been amiss. He had scrambled out of bed and out of the house in total darkness and in a hurry.

There was only one thing that made a sound like the one he had just heard.

And there was absolutely no chance it was coming from inside *his* house.

No, it was exhaustion. An auditory hallucination. Ears straining, picking up noises that did not exist.

Just as Ty was about to dismiss the sound he thought he had heard as a figment of an exhausted mind— clearly it was impossible—it came again. Louder. A babbling sound, like cold creek water tinkling over the first thin shards of ice.

And even though he was not a man with much experience in such things, Ty knew exactly what it was.

There was a baby inside his house.

Ty backed off his porch on silent feet, took a deep breath, felt a need to ground himself. He paused at the corner of his house, surveying the rolling land of the foothills, black against the midnight-blue of a rapidly darkening sky.

Snow-crusted pasture rolled away from him, beyond that a forested valley, all of it ringed by the craggy magnificence of the Rocky Mountains. The rugged sweep of his land soothed him, though it was not "safe." A man could die—or be injured—in this country fast and hard. The arrival of the cougar was a case in point, though getting wet and lost in December was far more danger-ous than an old mountain lion.

Still, for all its challenges, if ever a place was made to put a man's soul at ease, wasn't it this one? He had gone away from here once, and nearly lost himself.

The baby's happy squawking from inside the house was revving up a notch and he felt the simple shock of it down to his wet, frozen toes inside his boots.

A baby?

The truth be told, the danger of the cougar that had passed through his pastures appealed to him more than the mysterious presence of an infant inside his house.

Ty moved along the side of the house until he stood at the front. At the top of a long, long drive that twisted endlessly up the valley from Highway 22—sometimes called The Cowboy Trail—a car was parked in the gravel turnaround.

It was not the kind of car anyone in these parts would be caught dead driving.

No, folks around here favored pickup trucks, diesel, big enough to haul cattle and horses and hay. Trucks that could be shifted into four-wheel drive as the sea-sons changed and the roads became more demanding. People around here drove vehicles that were big, muddy and ugly.

No one Ty knew drove a car like this: bright red, shaped like a ladybug, impractically low to the ground.

*Cute.*

No surprise that a baby seat sat in the back, cheerfully padded with a bright fabric that had cartoon dogs and cats on it.

Ty placed his hand on the hood. Cold. The car had been here for a time.

He checked the plate. Alberta. A Calgary parking sticker was in the left-hand corner of the windshield. Not so far from wherever home was, then, maybe one and a half, two hours, if the roads had been good.

It would be easy enough to slide open the door and find the paperwork, but when he tried the door, it was locked. Under different circumstances he might have seen that as hilarious. Locked? He allowed his eyes to sweep the unpopulated landscape again. Against what?

He turned back to the house. Then he saw his front window.

For the second time in less than five minutes, Ty felt himself stumble backward in shock. His sense of being in an exhausted state of distorted reality increased. He made himself stand very still, squint through the sleet and snow, demanding *it* go away.

*It* was a Christmas tree. And it was real, because when he blinked hard and looked again, it was still there. Behind plate glass, bright lights winked against dark boughs, sent little splashes of color onto the gathering snow in his front yard.

He checked his driveway again, seeking familiar landmarks. Turned and studied his house, reassured himself that had been *his* pasture the cows had been shepherded into, *his* barn where he had put up his horse.

His eyes went back to the tree.

As far as Ty knew, there had never been one set up in the new Halliday house.

Or at least not in the twenty-six years he had lived here.

And in Ty's exhausted mind, a single, vulnerable hope crept in, a wish that he had made as a small boy.

*Maybe his mother had come home.*

He shook off the thought, irritated that it had somehow breached the wall of his adult world. Wishes were for children, and there had been no chance of his ever coming true, thanks to his father.

In his tired mind it did not bode well that the car in the yard, and the baby in his house, and the tree in his window had stirred something up that was better left alone, that he had not given any power to for years.

He went around to the back door again, habit more than anything else. In these parts the front door was rarely used, even by company. The back entrance was built to accommodate dirty boots and jackets, hats, gloves, bridles hung indoors in cold weather to keep the bits warm.

Ty Halliday took a deep breath, aware that the pit of his stomach felt exactly as it had in his days on the rodeo circuit when you gave that quick nod, the chute door opened, and suddenly you were riding a whirling explosion of bovine motion and malice.

He put his hand on the doorknob and felt it resist his flick of the wrist. At first he thought it was stuck, but then in an evening where he could have done without one more shock, he was shocked again. His door was locked.

Okay. Maybe one of his neighbors was playing a practical joke on him. Unlocked doors invited pranks. It was a tightly knit community and they all loved to have a laugh. Melvin Harris had once come home to find a burro in his living room. When Cathy Lambert had married Paul Cranston some of the neighbors had snuck into their house and filled every single drawer with confetti. They'd been married six years, and sometimes you still saw a piece of it sticking to one of Cathy's sweaters.

Ty lifted a worn welcome mat and found a rusty key. Sometimes he locked up if he was going to be away for a few days.

He slid the key in the door and let himself in, braced for some kind of battle, but what greeted him was enough to make him want to lay down his weapons.

His house, which he had always seen primarily as providing shelter, felt like *home*.

First, it smelled good. There was a light perfume in the air, woman, baby, underlying the smell of something wonderful cooking.

Second, the sound was enough to break every barrier a man had placed around his heart—and Ty would be the first to admit in his case, that was many. The baby was now chortling with glee.

Ty took the bridle he had slung over his shoulder and hung it on an empty peg. Then he took off his wet gloves and tossed them on the floor. He slid his sodden feet from muddy boots, and then took a deep breath—gladiator entering the ring to face unexpected horrors—and went up the stairs off the landing and surveyed his kitchen.

A fat baby with a shock of impossibly curly red hair sat dead center of Ty's kitchen on a blanket surrounded by toys. The baby, a boy, if the dump trucks and fire engines that surrounded him were any indication, was gurgling joyously.

The baby turned at his entrance, regarded him solemnly with gigantic soft brown eyes.

Instead of looking alarmed by the arrival of a big, irritated stranger, whose long Aussie-style riding coat was dripping water on the floor, the baby's eyes crinkled happily, and the joyous gurgling increased.

"Papa," he shouted.

Ty said a word he was pretty sure it was against the law to use in the presence of babies.

Or ladies.

Not that she looked like a lady, exactly. Through a wide archway, the kitchen opened onto the living room, and first a crop of hair as curly as the baby's appeared from behind the boughs of the tree. And then eyes, like the baby's, too, large and soft and brown, startled now.

Startled?

It was *his* house.

*Cute.* Just like the car. She had a light dusting of freckles across a delicate nose, curly hair the color of liquid honey in a jar. At first, he thought she had a boyish build, but Ty quickly saw her curves were just disguised in a masculine plaid shirt.

She didn't have on a speck of makeup and was one of those rare women who didn't need it, either.

"Who are you?" she demanded, a tiny tremor in her voice.

What kind of question was that to be asked in his own house? He could tell, from the way her eyes skittered around—looking for something to hit him with if he moved on the baby or her—that she was not just startled, she was scared. Any remaining thought that this might be a prank disappeared.

Her pulse beat frantically in the hollow of her slender neck.

Ty had to fight, again, the notion that he was somehow dreaming, and that he was going to wake up very soon. He didn't like it one little bit that exhaustion would make it way too easy to appreciate this scene.

That exhaustion was making some childhood wish try to push out of a dark corner of his mind.

Annoyed with himself—a man who believed in his strength and his determination, a man who put no faith at all in wishes—Ty planted his legs firmly apart, folded his arms over his chest.

She darted out from behind the tree, dropped the tangle of Christmas tree lights that were in her hand and grabbed a lamp. She yanked it off the side table and stood there holding it like a baseball bat.

Ty squinted at her. "Now, what are you going to do with that?" he asked mildly.

"If you touch my baby or me, you'll find out!"

The lamp was constructed out of an elk antler. It was big and heavy and it was already costing her to hold it up. It made him very aware of how small she was.

He had to fight to get beyond the exhaustion and the irritation that came with the weariness, to the same calm energy he tapped into to tame a nervous colt. He thought of the locked car and the locked back door.

He said, "I'm way more scared of a baby than that lamp. Especially one who calls me Papa."

He thought maybe her hold on the lamp relaxed marginally.

"How did you get into my house?" she demanded. "I locked the door."

"I used a key," he said, his voice deliberately quiet, firm, calm. "I happen to have one. I'm Ty Halliday. And last time I looked, this was my place."

The lamp wavered. Doubt played across her features for a second. Then she brought her weapon back up to batting position, glaring at him.

"Why don't you put that down?" he suggested. "Your arms are starting to shake. We both know I could take it from you if I had a mind to."

"Just try it," she warned him.

It was a little bit like an ant challenging an aardvark, but somehow he didn't think pointing that out to her was going to help the situation, and he reluctantly admired her spunk.

Something yanked on the hem of his coat. He looked down. The baby had crawled over and had grabbed a fistful of the wet oilskin of Ty's jacket. He was pulling himself up on it.

"Papa!" he crowed.

"Don't touch him!"

"Believe me, I'm not going to."

In a flash, she had set down the lamp, crossed the room, pried her baby's fist loose of his jacket and scooped him up into her arms.

This close he could smell them both. Her scent was subtle. Some flower. Lilac? No. Lavendar. It was mingled with baby powder. He wasn't sure how he recognized either of those scents, not common to his world, but he did, and it felt as if they were enveloping him.

She took a step back, eyeing him warily.

"You're in the wrong place," he said. "This really is my house. I'm cold and I'm wet and I'm dead tired, so let's get this sorted out so you can move on and I can go to bed."

Apparently the fact that he wanted to get rid of her rather than steal either her baby or her virtue reassured her in some way.

She pondered him. "If this is really your house, what's in the top drawer in the kitchen?"

"Knives and spoons and forks."

"That's in the top drawer of every kitchen!"

"You asked the question," he reminded her.

"Okay, second drawer."

He closed his eyes. "I'm losing patience," he warned her, but then gave in. The sooner he got that scared look off her face, the sooner she would realize her error and get on her way.

"Tea towels, once white, now the color of weak tea. One red oven glove with a hole burned right through it. Next drawer—potato masher, soup ladle, rolling pin, hammer for beating the tough out of rough cuts of beef."

Her eyes widened. "Oh, God," she whispered.

"How long have you been here that you know what's in my drawers?"

Her eyes shifted guiltily and made him wonder exactly what other drawers she had been investigating.

He swore softly. "Have you made it as far as my bedroom?"

"Oh, God," she said again.

The fear drained out of her, leaving her looking pale and shaky. She actually wobbled on her feet.

"Don't faint," he said. "I don't want to have to catch the kid."

"Oh," she said sharply, drawing herself up, annoyed,

"I am not going to faint. What kind of weak ninny do you take me for?"

"Weak ninny? How about the kind that reads *Jane Eyre?* How about the kind who is lost in the country, setting up housekeeping in someone else's house?" he said smoothly.

The truth was he liked her annoyance better than the pale, shaky look. He decided it would be good, from a tactical standpoint, to encourage annoyance.

"You don't look like you would know the first thing about *Jane Eyre,*" she said.

"That's right. Things are primitive out here in the sticks. We don't read and can barely write. When we do, we use a tablet and a chisel."

"I'm sorry," she said, blinking hard. "Now I've insulted you. I've moved in to the wrong house and I've insulted you. But I'm not going to faint. I promise. I'm not the fainting kind."

"Reassuring," he said drily. "And just for the record, I'm not easily insulted. It would take a lot more than the insinuation that I'm not up on my literary classics."

She sucked in a deep, steadying breath. "This isn't the McFinley residence, is it?"

Her face was crumpling, all the wariness and defiance seeping out of it. It was worse than pale and shaky.

He had the most ridiculous notion of wanting to comfort her, to move closer to her, pat her on the shoulder, tell her it would be all right.

But of course, he had no way of knowing if it would be all right, and he already knew if you moved too fast around a nervous colt, that little tiny bit of trust you had earned went out the window a whole lot faster than it had come in.

"But you know the McFinleys?" she asked, the desperation deepening in her voice. "I'm housesitting for them. For six months. They've left for Australia. They had to leave a few days before I could get away...."

He shook his head. He had the horrible feeling she was within a hairsbreadth of crying. Nervous colts were one thing. Crying women were a totally different thing. Totally.

The baby had sensed the change in his mother's tone. His happy babbling had ceased. He was eyeing his mother, his face scrunched up alarmingly, waiting for his cue.

One false move, Ty warned himself, and they would both be crying.

Ty checked the calendar in his mind. It was six days before Christmas. Why did a woman take her baby and find a new place to live six days before Christmas?

*Running.*

From what, or from whom, he told himself firmly, fell strictly into the none-of-his-business category.

"Mona and Ron?" Her voice faded as she correctly read his expression.

He was silent.

"You've never heard of them," she deduced. She sucked in another deep breath, assessing him.

Ty watched, trying not to let amusement tug at his mouth, as she apparently decided he was not an ax murderer, and made the decision to be brave.

She moved the baby onto her hip and wiped her

hand—she'd been scared enough to sweat?—on slacks that weren't made for riding horses. Like the shirt, the slacks emphasized the surprising lushness of such a slight figure.

All the defiance, all the I'll-lay-my-life-down-for-my-baby drained out of her. She looked wildly embarrassed at having been found making herself at home in someone else's house. Still, blushing, she tried for dignity as she extended her hand.

"I'm Amy Mitchell."

The blush made her look pretty. And vulnerable. He didn't want to take her hand, because despite her effort to be brave she still looked a breath away from crying, and the baby was still watching her intently, waiting.

"Mrs. Mitchell," he said, even though she wore no wedding band. He took her hand.

Ty knew instantly why he had resisted taking it. Amy Mitchell's hand in his felt tiny, soft beyond soft. The touch of her hand, his closeness to her, made him aware of his bleak world in ways that made him uncomfortable.

Her eyes were not brown, as he had initially thought from across the room, but a kaleidoscope of greens and golds, shot through with rich, dark hints of coffee color.

Now that she didn't feel she had her back against the wall, with a home invader coming at her, her eyes were soft and worried. Her honey-in-a-jar hair was scattered about her face in a wild disarray of curls that made him want to right it, to feel its texture beneath his fingertips.

Ty Halliday's world was a hard place. There was no softness in it, and no room for softness, either. There

was no room in his world for the tears that shone, un-
shed, behind the astounding loveliness of her eyes; there
was no room in his world for the bright, hopeful lights
of the Christmas tree.

The baby, eyes shifting from him to his mother and
back again, suddenly relaxed. "Papa," he cooed, and
leaned away from his mommy, reaching for Ty.

Ty took a defensive step backward.

There was no room in his world for such innocence
or trust. All these things were as foreign to Ty as an ex-
otic, unvisited land.

He realized he was still holding Amy Mitchell's hand.
She realized it, too, and with a deepening blush, slipped
it from his.

"I can't believe this," she muttered. "I have GPS."

She said that as if her faulty system or reading of it
was the cause of the stain moving up her cheeks, instead of her awareness of him.

And maybe it was.

But he didn't think so.

Still, he focused on the GPS, too, something safe in
a room that suddenly seemed fraught with dangers of
a kind he had never considered before.

The faith city folk put in their gadgets never failed to
astound him, but aware she was still terrifyingly close
to the tear stage, he tried to think of a way to phrase it
that wouldn't wound her.

"It wouldn't be the first time GPS got people into
trouble in this country," he said after some thought.

"Really?"

Obviously, she was pleased that hers was not an isolated case of being misled by her global positioning system, and he could have left it at that.

Instead, he found the worry lines dissolving on her forehead encouraging enough to want to make them— and the possibility of tears—disappear altogether.

"One of the neighbors found an old couple stranded in George's Pass last year. They'd been on the news. Missing for a week."

But instead of being further reassured that her mistake was not all that uncommon, Amy looked aghast. He remembered the locked doors and saw her considering other scenarios. Disastrous possibilities flashed through her eyes as she considered what could have happened to her if she had followed her GPS instructions somewhere other than his driveway.

Which just served as a reminder that he could not really be trusted with soft things or a woman so frightened of life she locked everything all the time and was ready to defend herself with a lamp if need be.

She marshaled herself and turned away from him. She plunked the baby down on his padded rear and began to whip around the room, picking up baby things, putting them in a pile. Given the short amount of time she had been here, the pile grew to a mountain with astonishing swiftness.

"I'm terribly sorry, Mr. Halliday. We'll go right away. I'm so embarrassed."

If he had thought she was blushing before, that had only been a hint of the main event.

Amy Mitchell was turning a shade of red that matched some of the lights on the tree. Was that a smile tickling around the edges of his mouth? He tried to remember the last time he had smiled.

*Sunshine Sketches of a Little Town* had made him smile, he decided. He'd reread that a week or so ago.

No doubt his current good cheer was because his visitor was so intent on leaving. There was no need to tell her to pack her baby and get the hell out of his house. She was doing it all on her own.

"It will take me a minute to gather my things," she said, all business and flurrying activity. "I'll leave the groceries."

"Groceries?"

"Oh, I stocked the fridge. I thought I was going to be living here, after all."

"You're not leaving the groceries," he said.

"Oh, no, really. You didn't have a thing in your fridge. That's part of why I thought I was in the right place. Nothing in the fridge, no tree up, no socks on the floor."

She *had* been in his bedroom.

"Really, I didn't think anyone had lived here recently." She shot him a look that was faintly accusing and faintly sympathetic. "It certainly didn't look as though anyone lived here."

"I don't need your groceries," he said a bit more tightly than he intended. He was so hungry, and whatever she had in the fridge would be better than the tin of stew he had planned on opening. But to admit that might invite more sympathy, and he definitely didn't need her sympathy.

So his place looked unlived in. So it wasn't going to be the featured house on *Cozy Country Homes*. So what? It was a place to hang his hat and lay his head. He didn't need more than that.

Or at least he hadn't felt as if he had for a long, long time. But there it was again, unwanted, uninvited emotion whispering along his spine.

*Yearning.* A wish he had managed to bury deep to have something that he did not have.

"I started to unpack. I've got some things in the bedroom," she explained as she scurried around the room, the remnants of her embarrassment making her awkward. She dropped a baby puzzle on the floor, and the wooden pieces scattered.

He just knew she had been in there, in his bedroom. And he knew, suddenly, why it bothered him, too. That could move yearning in a whole other direction if he let it, which he wasn't going to.

He hadn't allowed himself feelings for a long, long time. It must be the Christmas tree, the baby, the scents, the astonishing discovery of a woman in his house, his own exhaustion, making him oddly vulnerable, making him aware of a hole a mile deep where his soul should be.

He watched Amy Mitchell, on her hands and knees, picking up the pieces of the puzzle, stuffing them into a box. Out of the corner of his eye he could see the baby roll off his rear end onto all fours.

With startling speed and unsettling determination, he crawled across the floor, making a beeline for Ty.

Ty stepped out of his way. The baby followed like a heat-seeking missile locked on target.

"Papa!" he yelled.

"Where is his papa?" he asked, deftly sidestepping the baby one more time.

# CHAPTER TWO

"So, that's what they call the Texas two-step," Amy said, rocking back on her heels to watch, after something in Ty's tone had made her look up from where she was gathering the puzzle pieces.

"It's not funny. Tell him to stop it."

But it was funny, watching the big cowboy trying, not without desperation, to evade the determined baby. She giggled.

The cowboy glanced at her, glared, shifted away from the baby. "Don't laugh," he warned her.

"I'm sorry. It just looks as if you'd be completely unfazed by almost anything life threw at you. And you're running from a baby!"

"I am not running," he said tersely. "Call him off."

She did laugh then. Ty glared at her, stepped away from the baby. He had waltzed around half the living room.

"Just stop and pick him up," Amy managed to advise between snorts of laughter. "He thinks it's a game."

Oh, it felt good to laugh. She knew it was partly reaction to the situation she found herself in, a release from the fear she had felt when she had been startled by the big cowboy appearing in a home she'd already been busy making hers. But life had been such a serious affair for far too long.

The tall cowboy glaring at her warningly only seemed to make it more impossible to control her rising mirth.

"Now you want me to pick him up? Before you were going to hit me with a lamp if I even looked at him."

"That was when I thought you were the intruder," she said, wiping at her eyes. "Now I know it's me who is the intruder. If you pick him up and cuddle him for a few seconds, he'll lose interest."

*"Cuddle?"*

"You mustn't say that as if I'm asking you to get friendly with a rattlesnake!"

"It was the word *cuddle* that I took offense to!"

"A threat to your masculinity, is it?"

"I'm wet. I'm dirty."

"You're scared."

He looked at her darkly, and then heaved a sigh.

"Terrified," he admitted, and the laughter, recently tamed, burst free again. It still felt good to release the tension that had been building in her since Ty Halliday had set her world upside down by coming in the back door of the house she had been assuming was going to be all hers for the next six months.

The tiniest smile tugged at the edges of that hard mouth, and her laughter died. Nothing in her entire existence—she'd lived all over the world, gone to university, married into a well-to-do society family—had prepared her for a man like Ty Halliday.

In a world filled with illusions, the man was absolutely, one hundred per cent real. He had physical power and presence. He was as big as an oak tree, and just as solid. He had seemed to fill the room, to charge the air in it with a subtle hiss of dark sensuality. There was something about him standing there, all cowboy, that was equal parts menace and romance.

There was toughness in the chiseled angles of his dark whisker-shadowed face, something uncompromising about the set of his chin, the muscle that jerked along his jawline, the hard lack of humor around the line of his lips.

He was handsome—Amy was not sure she had ever seen eyes that color, a flinty blue sapphire—almost beyond words, but his good looks were of the untouchable variety. He wore solitude, self-reliance, as comfortably as he wore that past-his-knees, dark, dripping Australian-style riding coat that emphasized the broadness of his shoulders and the impossible length of his legs.

"If you pick him up, the chasing-papa game will be over," she said, though suddenly she was not at all sure she wanted to see her baby in those strong arms.

She needn't have worried. Ty Halliday was not picking up anyone's baby. He stepped away, Jamey followed, crowing demandingly.

"At least stop and pat him on the head and say hello to him. His name is Jamey, with a *Y*."

"The *Y* part is important?"

"Very important," she said solemnly. It marked one of the few occasions she had stood up to her husband and her in-laws. They had wanted James. She had not. She had thought *Jamey* was a wonderful compromise. They had not. But for once, she had stood firm.

"Just try it," she said encouragingly.

Ty stopped, contemplated the situation. Jamey pitched himself into the hesitation, grabbed the hem of the wet coat and pulled himself up.

"Papa."

Looking very much as if he was reaching out to a full-grown tiger, Ty rested a reluctant hand on Jamey's nest of red curls.

"Hey. Little fella. Jamey."

"Papa," Jamey crooned, leaned into the jacket without letting go, and plopped his thumb in his mouth.

"Why does he think I'm his papa, for heaven's sake?"

"Don't take it personally. He calls every man that."

"Why? Where is his papa?"

Ty looked at her then, and his gaze seemed uncomfortably all-seeing.

"Are you running from something?" he asked softly.

She actually shivered from the fierce look that crossed his face. She told herself not to take it personally. He would just be one of those men with a very traditional set of values, thinking women and children—much as he disliked the latter—were in need of his extremely masculine self for protection.

Amy hated that the old-fashioned notion actually filled her with the oddest sense of comfort.

"What would make you think I'm running from something?" she hedged, because of course that was uncomfortably close to the truth.

"Less than a week before Christmas, and you're looking for a new home?"

"It's just the timing," she said. "The McFinleys wanted to be in Australia by Christmas."

He did not look convinced, but he did not look as if he cared to pursue it, either.

"Where's his papa?" he asked again, patting Jamey—who was showing absolutely no sign of losing interest in him—with surprising gentleness, on the head.

"I'm a widow," she said quietly. "Jamey's father was killed in an accident three months after he was born. It's nearly nine months ago now."

Some shadow passed over his face and through the depths of those amazing sapphire eyes. She felt as if Ty Halliday could clearly see the broken place in her.

She could feel his awkwardness. It was obvious from his house that he was a man alone in the world, and had been for a long time. There was not a single feminine touch in this place. It was also obvious he was a man allergic to attachments. There were no pictures, no family photographs. There was no ring on his finger.

On arriving, she had thought the McFinleys had taken their personal touches down so that she could put up her own and feel more at home. But she had not even asked herself about the unlocked door, the lack of curtains, or throw rugs or little lace dollies. She had not asked herself about the dresser still filled with neatly folded clothes.

Now, feeling his eyes on her, Amy knew it was way beyond this solitary cowboy's skill level to know what to say to her. She was touched when he tried.

"That seems to fall squarely into the life-is-unfair department," he said gently.

She lifted her chin. "I stopped expecting life to be fair a long time ago."

He frowned. "No, you didn't."

"Pardon me?"

"That sounds like something I would say. And you're not like me."

"And what are you like?"

"Cynical. World-weary."

"That's me exactly!" she protested.

A small smile teased the devastating curve of his lips. "No, it's not," he said. "You just wish it was. It's evident from looking at you, you are nothing of the sort."

"You can't possibly know that about me on such a short acquaintance."

"Yes, I can."

"How?" she demanded, folding her arms over her chest, some defense against what he was seeing. No, what he *thought* he was seeing.

She was not the naive girl she had once been, so reliant on the approval of others, begging for love, so desperate for a place to call home that it had made her overlook things she should have seen. Amy Mitchell was on a new path now.

She was going to be fully independent. She was not going to rely on anyone else to make a home for her and her baby.

Looking after the McFinley house, venturing so far from the familiar, expanding her website, Baby Bytes, into a viable business from there, were all part of her new vision for her life.

She hated it that a complete stranger thought he could see through it.

She hated it even more that her first day of her new life was turning into something of a fiasco.

Thankfully, no one but Ty Halliday ever needed to know.

She had called her in-laws as soon as she stepped in the door to let them know she had arrived safely.

She had heard her mother-in-law's disapproval, so like her son's had been.

"For heaven's sake, Amy, give up this harebrained scheme. John and I are delighted to look after you and Jamey. Delighted."

Delighted to control and criticize her, just like their son had done. Delighted to keep her dependent on them. She shivered. Wouldn't they love to see the predicament she was in now?

But they never had to know. In a little while she would be where she was supposed to be, none the worse for the wear, no one to question her competence.

"By the way," she said, "before I forget, I owe you money for a phone call. My cell phone wouldn't work here. Now, how can you know so much about me?"

"No one with a truly jaded soul would offer me money for a phone call I wouldn't even know you made for a month. And no one truly fed up with life arrives at a new home and makes it their first priority to put up a Christmas tree," he said.

"Oh."

"I don't even know where you found this stuff. The tree is obviously too big to have arrived in your shrimpy little car."

That shrimpy little car was the first major purchase she had ever made on her own. Her mother-in-law, not aware that Baby Nap had just signed up to be a sponsor on the website, had not thought it was a sensible use of funds.

"I prefer to think of it as sporty," Amy said proudly. The car was part of the new independent her!

"Sporty. Shrimpy. There is no way a Christmas tree arrived in the trunk of it."

"The tree was in your basement."

He turned and scanned her face, looking for a lie. "This tree was in *my* basement?"

"Along with all the decorations and lights and such."

"No kidding." He whistled, long and low. "Who would buy an artificial tree when there are a million real ones two steps out the back door?"

"So you usually have a real tree?" she asked.

He snorted. "We've never had a tree up in this house."

"But why?" she whispered, horrified by his revelation.

He looked at her and shook his head. "You want me to believe you're cynical when you cannot imagine a world with no Christmas tree, a world without fluffy white kittens, a world without fresh baked chocolate chip cookies?"

"Is it for religious reasons?" she asked solemnly.

He threw back his head and laughed then, but it was not a nice laugh.

"Religion is as foreign to this house as Christmas trees. And now, Miss Cynical, you look like you took a wrong turn and ended up in the devil's den."

At least he had dropped the *Mrs.*

Amy was aware she should let it go. And couldn't. "I just can't believe you never had a Christmas tree. Why?"

"It wasn't a big deal. My mom left when I was about

the same age as your little guy. It was just me and my dad. Christmas was just another day, filled with hard work and the demands of the ranch."

She felt appalled, and it must have shown on her face.

"Don't get me wrong. The neighbors always had us for dinner."

That did not make her feel any less appalled. "Your mom left you?" She knew she shouldn't have asked, but she couldn't help it. She thought of what it would take to make her leave Jamey.

And the only answer she could come up with was death.

He was irritated by her question, and it was clear he had no intention of answering her. He rolled his shoulders, and she could tell he hated that he had said anything about himself that might be construed as inviting sympathy. She offered it nonetheless.

"I guess I'm not the only one life has been unfair to," she said softly into his silence.

He wouldn't look at her. He shook free of Jamey, again and moved over, looked in one of the boxes. He shuffled through some old ornaments and a Christmas tree star.

And then he took his hand out and stared at it.

He was holding a packet of letters, yellow with age, tied with a blue ribbon. He swore, his voice a low, animal growl of pain.

Amy froze, stared at him wide-eyed.

"Sorry," he muttered, and rubbed his brow with a tired hand. "Sorry."

"What's wrong?" she asked, and she knew instantly,

from the way his expression closed, that he couldn't bear it that she could see something was wrong.

He shoved the letters into a deep pocket on his jacket.

"I've just come home from a real devil of a day to find my house invaded by a lamp-wielding stranger with a baby who wants to call me Papa. What's wrong? Why, nothing!"

"I'm sorry," Amy said. "I really am. I'm leaving as fast as I can."

And she meant it.

There was something about him that was so alone it made her ache. It made her want to lay her hand on the thickness of that powerful wrist and say to him, *Tell me.*

But if he did, if he ever confided in her, she knew instinctively it would change something irrevocably and forever.

Like her plan for a new life.

Still, looking into his closed face, she knew she was in no danger from his confidences.

He kept things to himself.

He did not lean.

He did not rely.

He was the last of a dying breed, a ruggedly independent man who was entirely self-sufficient, confident in his own strength to be enough to get him by in an unforgiving environment.

He was totally alone in the world, and he liked it that way.

She was leaving. She did not need to know one more single thing about him.

He moved to the window, away from Jamey's relentless pursuit. He looked out and sighed.

"I don't think life is quite done being unfair to either one of us," he said, his voice deep, edged with gravel and gruffness.

"What do you mean?"

"Come and see for yourself."

Amy moved beside him and was stunned to see that while she had been decorating the tree, oblivious, a storm had deepened outside the window. The snow was mounding on his driveway, like heaps of fresh whipped cream. Already the gravel road that twisted up to the house was barely discernible from the land around it.

His eyes still on the window, not looking at her, he said, "Mrs. Mitchell?"

"Amy."

"Whatever. You won't be going anywhere tonight."

"Not going anywhere tonight?" Amy echoed. But she *had* to. She had to correct her mistake, hopefully before anyone else found out.

The urgency to do so felt as if it intensified the moment he said she wasn't going anywhere.

If there was one thing Amy Mitchell was through with, it was being controlled. It was somebody telling her what to do. It was being treated as an inferior rather than an equal.

And she fully intended to make that clear to Mr. Ty Halliday. He wasn't going to tell her what to do.

"I *have* to go," she said.

"This isn't the city. Going out in that isn't quite the same as going to the corner store for a jug of milk. If you get in trouble—"

"And you think I will."

"—and I think there's a chance you might, it can turn deadly."

She shivered at that.

"There's not a lot of people out here waiting to rescue you if you go in the ditch or off the road, or get lost some more or run out of gas."

"I'm a very good driver," she said. "I've been driving in winter conditions my whole life."

"*Urban* winter conditions," he guessed, and made no effort to hide his scorn. "I don't think that's a chance you want to take with your baby."

"You're probably overstating it."

"Why would I do that?" he asked, and his eyebrows shot up in genuine bewilderment.

Yes, why would he? He had made it plain her and Jamey's being here was an imposition on him. The possibility startled her that he wasn't trying to control her, that he was only being practical.

"The native people have lived in this country longer than both of us," he continued quietly. "When they see this kind of weather, they just stop wherever they are and make the best of it. They don't think about where they want to be or what time they should be there and who might be waiting for them. They stay in the moment and its reality and that's why they don't end up dead the way somebody who is married to their agenda might."

Amy saw, reluctantly, how right he was. This was the kind of situation that had made her husband, Edwin, mental. And her in-laws. Delayed flights. Dinner late. Any wrench in their carefully laid plans sent them off the deep end.

This was her new life. If she just applied the same

old rules—if she rigidly adhered to her plan—wasn't she going to get the same old thing? Feeling uptight and harried and like she had somehow failed to be perfect?

What if instead she saw this as an opportunity to try something new, a different approach to life? What if she relaxed into what life had given her rather than trying to force it to meet her vision and expectation?

What if she acted as if she was free? What if she just made the best of whatever came?

Her desire to protest, to have her own way, suddenly seemed silly and maybe even dangerous, so she let it dissipate.

And when it was gone, she looked at Ty Halliday, standing in the window, his coat drawn around him, his handsome face remote, and she was not sure she had ever seen anyone so alone.

At any time of year, that probably would have struck her as poignant.

But at Christmas?

What did it mean that he had never put up a Christmas tree, not even when he was a child? That seemed unbearably sad to her, and intensified that sense she had of him being terribly and absolutely alone in the world.

What if she used these altered circumstances to make the best of it? What if she made the best of it by giving him an unexpected gift? What if she overcame her own hurt, the unfairness of her own life, and gave this stranger a gift?

A humble gift. A decorated tree.

Wasn't that really what Christmas was all about? When she had left the safety of her old world behind her this morning, she hadn't been running away from something, as he had guessed.

No, she hoped she was running toward something. Hadn't she hoped she was moving toward something she had lost? Some truth about who she really was? Or maybe about who she wanted to be? About the kind of life she wanted to give her baby?

She did not want to be so wrapped up in her own grievances she could not be moved by the absolute aloneness of another human being.

She took a deep breath.

"Okay," she said, "I guess I could stay. Just for the night."

He turned and looked at her, one eyebrow lifted, as if amused she thought she had a choice.

"In the morning," he said with the annoying and quiet confidence of a man who was accustomed to being deferred to, "I'll see that you get where you're going."

*I'll look after you.*

Maybe it was the fury of the storm that made that seem attractive. Or maybe, Amy thought, she had an inherent weakness in her character that made her want to be looked after!

"I can clearly see it makes sense to avoid going out in the storm tonight, but no thank you to your offer to show me the way in the morning. I am quite capable of looking after myself."

The wind gusted so strongly that it rattled the glass of the window, hurled snow against it. Nature, in its unpredictable wrath, was reminding her that some things were going to be out of her control.

But not, she reminded herself, how she handled those

things. And so she would be a better person and finish decorating this tree, her gift to a stranger, before she left here tomorrow and never looked back. It would not matter to her if he didn't show appreciation.

Somewhere in his heart he would feel the warmth of the tree and the gesture, and be moved by it.

She slid him another glance, and saw the man was dead on his feet. And that he was soaked from the top of his dripping cowboy hat to his wet socks. He hadn't driven up in a vehicle.

"You were out in that," she said, and was ashamed by how thoroughly she had made it all about her.

He glanced at her and seemed to find her concern amusing. "That's my world," he said with a touch of wryness. "Besides, it wasn't that bad then."

"You're starving," she guessed. "And frozen."

He said nothing, a man accustomed to discomfort, to pitting his strength against whatever the world brought him, and expecting to win. Ty Halliday was obviously a man entirely used to looking after himself.

So, since she was stuck here anyway, she would make the best of it, and this would become part of her gift to him.

"I've got a chicken potpie in the oven. I'll make a salad while you go shower. Everything should be ready in twenty minutes."

Her take-charge tone of voice was probably spoiled somewhat by the fire she felt creep up her cheeks after she mentioned the shower.

The very thought of him in the shower, steam rising off a body that she could tell was hard-muscled and powerful, made something hot and sweet and wildly uncomfortable unfold inside of her.

He regarded her for a moment too long. She suspected he wanted to refuse even this tiniest offer to enter his world. But then he sniffed the air like a hungry wolf and surrendered to the fact she was already in his world. He turned away.

"Thanks," he said gruffly. "It smells good."

She could tell it was not easy for him to accept her offer, but obviously, like her, he knew he had to just try and make the best of an awkward situation.

He went by her, and his scent overrode that of the potpie in the oven. He smelled of wet oilskin, wild horses, pure man, and his aroma enveloped her. And then he was gone. Amy waited until she heard a door down the hallway snap shut before she went and sank down on her knees beside her baby. She was aware her knees were trembling.

The wrong house?

Her clothes, her partially unpacked suitcase, were spread out on Ty Halliday's bed!

It all seemed as if it might be a terrible omen. She had set out on the road this morning to a brand-new life.

She had not listened to the objections of her family or her in-laws.

She was done with the stuffiness of it all. She was done with being stifled. Lectured. Patronized.

This morning, she had felt joy unfurl in her for the first time in a long time. Amy had followed her heart instead of her head.

But where had it led her?

Amy tried to still the trembling of her knees and her heart by picking up Jamey and settling him on her lap.

"Papa?" he asked, a plaintive whisper, his eyes glued to the place where Ty Halliday had disappeared down the hallway.

"No, sweetie, not Papa." There was no sense telling Jamey, yet again, there was no papa. In all his nearly a year of wisdom, even though his father had been gone for longer than he had been in Jamey's life, Jamey had become determined to have what his little pals at play school had—a daddy.

"Papa," Jamey insisted, leaning back into her and putting his thumb in his mouth.

Amy heard the shower turn on in another part of the house and was horrified to feel a heated blush move up her cheeks.

Good grief! She had set out this morning on a mission. To find herself. Her real self. Who she was genuinely meant to be.

She could not let the first obstacle—no matter that he was large and intimidating—make her feel as if she was on the wrong road!

She had to act the part of the confident woman she was determined to become. That woman ran her own business and her own house and was not always flinching from put-downs.

Amy refused to go any further down that road, feeling guilty as always, for acknowledging she might not have been completely satisfied with the life her husband had given her.

Out loud, quietly, she said, "I will not be a schoolgirl who blushes at the thought of a man in the shower."

But, of course, the man in that shower was not any man.

Could anything prepare a woman for the kind of raw magnetism Ty Halliday radiated?

Could anything prepare a woman for a man who moved with such unconscious grace, as fluid as water, so at home with his own power? Could anything prepare a woman for that kind of pure masculine energy, the kind that felt like a force field around him, sizzling, faintly but alluringly dangerous?

Could anything prepare a woman for the strength that radiated out from under the brim of that soaked hat, from underneath that wet slicker like a palpable force?

The answer was no.

But she reminded herself firmly of her mission.

Tomorrow she would be back on the right road. Tonight she would decorate that tree as her gift to a stranger. She would cook him a hot meal. That was it.

Tomorrow her quest would resume. She was on a journey. She was determined to find out who she really was, and what really mattered. She had lost sight of both things since her marriage.

And Ty Halliday was just an uncomfortable—and brief—detour from that quest. Amy put down her baby and went to rummage through Ty's ill-equipped kitchen.

Amy made a vow. She resolved not to let his shocking appeal alter her focus. She put Jamey on his blanket surrounded by his toys and checked the chicken potpie she'd put in the oven earlier for their supper.

She frowned. The pie was not cooking properly, and she suspected the oven was not producing the correct heat for the temperature it was set at. She turned it up, and the oven made a protesting noise. The oven seemed decidedly cranky.

"Just like its owner," she muttered.

"Papa," Jamey supplied.

"Precisely." And then she realized she could not start agreeing, even casually, with Jamey labeling Ty as his papa.

"Don't call him that, sweetie. He's not your papa."

"Umpa?"

"No, not your grandpa, either. Call him—" The oven made another noise, and she went and opened the door and peered in. The burner was red-hot and making a hissing sound.

"Oh, damn," she said, and turned it back down.

"Odam," Jamey repeated.

"Sure," she said distractedly, "call him that."

The oven looked after, and papa renamed something Jamey could pronounce, Amy turned to the salad.

In every place in the world where her family had moved to, Amy, to her career-oriented mother's bewilderment, had always found sanctuary in the kitchen. She loved to cook.

As she was ripping and washing lettuce, she heard the water shut off in the bathroom and had a renegade thought about naked wet skin and steam.

And then, as if her thoughts were too hot to handle, the smoke alarm started to shriek.

She turned from the sink to see smoke was roiling out of the oven.

Jamey, startled, began to wail along with the smoke alarm.

Amy donned the red oven mitt with the hole burned

right through it, and opened the oven door a crack. Just as she had suspected, the potpie had boiled over onto the burner.

She shut the oven off and slammed the door. She opened the kitchen window, and picked up her howling baby.

"Hey. Hey, little man, it's okay."

But it wasn't. Because just then, through the haze of smoke that filled the kitchen, Ty appeared.

Ty scanned the room, every muscle taut. Amy could have sworn he was prepared to lay down his life for her and Jamey, two near strangers. A strange emotion clawed at her throat.

Then, when Ty saw there was no emergency, he stood down. Instantly. He went from ready to relaxed in a second, though a certain level of annoyance marred his altogether too handsome features.

But while Ty relaxed, Amy felt as if her nerve endings were singing with tension. It wasn't just that he had been prepared to lay down his life for them, either.

No, Ty Halliday was nearly naked, clad only in boxer shorts.

And if the smoke alarm had not been going off before, it certainly would have started now. Because Ty Halliday was nearly naked. Even his feet were sexy!

He was everything she had imagined he would be, only about a hundred times off the scale of where her imagination went to.

His dark slashing eyebrows, the dark shadow of whiskers on his face, had made her think his hair would be dark under the cowboy hat he had worn.

But he was blond, his wet hair the color of antique pieces of gold in a just opened treasure chest.

But the astonishing color of his hair held her attention for only a millisecond. He was lean and strong and his skin was flawless. His arms, corded with muscles of honed steel, were deeply tanned, a color that didn't go away, apparently, even in these long days of winter. His legs were equally powerful-looking: long, straight, made to curve around a horse, or a bucking bull, or…

She couldn't go there. Instead, she let her hungry gaze go to his chest, deep and smooth. His shoulders were impossibly broad and his stomach a perfect washboard of rippling, hard muscle. Ty was just way too hot to handle, and as the smoke detector continued to shriek, Amy was aware her own five-alarm fire had started going off deep inside of her.

She dared look at the boxers. Her mouth fell open.

Ty Halliday was wearing bright red boxer shorts, low, snugged over his flat hips and the taut lines of his lower belly. And what were his red boxer shorts covered with?

Santa, his sleigh and twelve reindeer. She presumed twelve reindeer, because she really shouldn't count.

She didn't want to appear too interested, but she could not draw her eyes away until she had read the words that were also dancing across the shorts.

*Have you been naughty or nice?*

For the second time that day, she started to laugh. She laughed so hard the tears squirted from her eyes.

Or maybe that was the smoke.

Ty folded those gorgeous muscled arms over an equally gorgeous muscled chest, planted his long, muscled legs far apart.

If it weren't for the shorts, he would definitely have the intimidating presence she was fairly certain he was aiming for.

"I don't see what's so funny," he yelled over the screaming alarm, the baby howling and her laughter.

"You don't?" she gasped.

"No, I don't," he said sternly.

"Ty Halliday, you have some Christmas spirit, after all." She pointed. "You just keep it well hidden."

# CHAPTER THREE

Ty followed her pointing finger, unfolded his arms and looked down at himself.

He said three words in a row that made the baby stop yelling for a moment, and stare at him with wide-eyed wariness.

He would have appreciated a little wide-eyed wariness from Amy, but she was smirking mirthfully.

"Oh, my," she said silkily. "Are you blushing?"

"No." He folded his arms again, leveled a warning look at her, which she ignored.

"Yes, you are."

"You're bluffing. There's no way you can tell through all this smoke what color my face is. But you can take my word for it, Amy, I haven't blushed since I was ten or eleven years old."

Amy. He contemplated that. How had Mrs. Mitchell become Amy so quickly?

Marching by her with as much dignity as he could muster, Ty grabbed a towel from the drawer he had described to her earlier. He went and stood under the smoke detector and flailed at it until the rush of air created by the tea towel infused it with enough fresh air to shut off.

Still laughing, she went across the kitchen, scooped up the baby and covered his tearstained face with kisses. He hiccupped several times, and then stopped crying, abruptly, as if someone had pulled a switch.

The silence was blessed.

"Don't believe him," she told the baby. "Nobody *stops* blushing when they're eleven. That's when they start."

Ty ordered himself not to show the slightest curiosity. But, despite the order, he heard himself saying skeptically, "You remember what made you blush at eleven?"

"Of course."

He ordered himself not to pursue it. He heard himself say, "And?"

"The cruelty of boys, of course. First bra. The back strap being snapped."

He did not want to be thinking about her with her first bra. Or any bra at all. But once a man's mind went to those places it was tougher than wrestling an ornery steer to bring it back in line.

*Black and slinky? Red and sexy? White and sporty?* He hardened his features as she squinted at him.

"You're right," she decided. "I don't think you are blushing. So, what made you stop blushing at the tender age of eleven?"

He was standing in his kitchen in his underwear, being encouraged to exchange confidences with a perfect stranger. He ordered himself to go get dressed.

Instead, he said, "I was raised by a man, around a family of men, a couple of old ranch hands who were as tough and as hard as two buckets of old nails. The hands seemed to consider it part of their job to educate me, no matter how embarrassing the information they imparted was.

"I was toughened up on incessant teasing, prank-pulling and roughhousing. Those guys considered it their sacred and sworn duty to ferret out any form of weakness in me and snuff it out before it blossomed. Believe me, by the time I was ten or eleven, I'd learned absolute control over my reactions to everything."

He'd said way too much. She looked horrified and fascinated, as if she had met a man raised by wolves.

Which, of course, was probably not that far off the mark.

So, no, he knew he was not blushing. Though if ever a situation called for embarrassment it was this one!

Ty had just stepped out of the shower when he'd heard the smoke detector going off. He'd gone into rescue mode, some deep instinct he didn't know he had kicking in. There was a baby and a woman in his house, and if the place was on fire, he had to get them out.

But even in hero mode, he wasn't running out there naked.

And so he'd opened his bottom drawer—he was into the stuff he *never* wore because he hadn't gotten at the laundry for a while—and randomly picked something to shove on.

Now, his adrenaline still pumping, even though it was obvious his house was not on fire and no one needed him to be a hero, he looked down at his choice of attire again.

He said the three words again. Jamey commenced howling.

Amy and Jamey gave him identical looks of accusation, though hers was tempered by that tiny smile that wouldn't quit, and that kept drawing Ty's eyes back to the full, luscious curve of her plump bottom lip.

"Oh, I get it," she said. "You swear instead of blush. Very manly."

She was being sarcastic!

"There, there," she said, patting the baby's plump shoulder. It seemed it would be ineffectual against the tears and hollering, but both subsided almost instantly, and Jamey burrowed deep into his mother's shoulder.

Then he peered at Ty with yet more accusation, put his thumb in his mouth and took a long pull on it.

"Odam," he said through his thumb, and then slurped contentedly.

"See?" Ty said approvingly. "It's what men do. They swear. Your baby just said 'damn.'"

"He did not swear!" she said indignantly.

"Mild, but still a cuss. Good boy."

"Stop it. He wasn't cursing. I think he may be calling on the Viking god."

"Ha! You're telling me your baby is versed in Viking mythology?" Ty realized he was enjoying this little interchange.

She shrugged as if it was a possibility. That damned smile was still tickling along the luscious lines of her lips.

"I mean, I'm all for embracing Viking ways," he said. "No Christmas."

"Tell your shorts you don't like Christmas." She looked as though she was going to start laughing again. Her laughter was one of the nicest sounds he had ever heard. He felt it could be like a drug, making him weak when he needed to be strong.

But even so, a man had to defend himself. "Just to set the record straight, for your information, I didn't buy these for myself. We do a gift exchange with the neighbors. It's mostly gag gifts."

"All right," she said soothingly, "I get it. Christmas spirit only by accident in the Halliday household."

He nodded his confirmation. "And just while I'm setting the record straight, his name is Odin."

She looked baffled.

"The Norse god, worshipped by the Vikings. Odin. Not Odam."

Her mouth fell open.

He knew he had said quite enough, but he didn't even bother ordering himself to stop, because he felt as if he couldn't.

"Also, while we're setting the record straight, I'm not just some dumb cowboy who fell off the hay wagon yesterday."

Why was he saying this? She didn't need to know this!

Obviously, there had been no one around except the horses and cows to talk to for a very long time. Too long. His mouth felt as if it was running like a river that had been let loose of a dam.

"I read," he said, "I read all the time. I read everything I can get my hands on."

"Have you really read *Jane Eyre?*"

He wasn't going to stand here in his underwear making confessions about his reading material. He felt annoyed enough with himself that he had told her something so integral to who he was.

There it was again, his childhood, rising like a ghost. A lonely little boy longing for his mother, reading his pain away despite the fact that he had been teased unmercifully for it. It had never stopped him, though, maybe even driven him deeper into his passion for books.

When he said nothing, her eyes went round. "You have!"

He said nothing, turned on his heel, went into his room and got dressed. If he chose more carefully than normal, he wasn't admitting that to anyone, least of all not himself.

Dinner was delicious, ambrosia to a man who ate out of a can and a freezer, unless one of the neighbors took pity on him and delivered a casserole. Ty had ordered himself not to say one more revealing thing to Amy, but he needn't have worried. She didn't bring up the subject of his reading material.

She had her hands full with the baby. Ty did not have a great deal of experience being around babies, eating, or otherwise.

Ty had no high chair in his house, so the squirming Jamey was on his mother's lap, seemingly doing his best to dodge the spoon his mother held for him and eat with his hands.

Between food being thrown on the floor to exuberant shouts of "oops" and food being smashed to a chant of "Odam," the baby kept his mother hopping and Ty thoroughly entertained.

"Wow," Ty said, when the baby's bowl was finally

empty. "I don't know if any of that got in his mouth. There's goo in his ears, eyes and nose, and between his toes, and all over you, but as far as I could see not a single crumb made it to his mouth. Not that he looks undernourished."

She brushed crumbs off her blouse and shook them out of her hair, then rose, baby on her hip, and began to clear plates.

"Stop it. I'll do that."

For a moment, she looked as if she was going to pro-test, but then she looked at the baby, and his head-to-toe covering of chicken potpie.

"Are you sure you don't mind? I could pop him in the bath before bed. You don't mind if I put him in your tub?"

"Of course not. Thank you for the dinner. It was the best thing I've had in a long time."

"You're welcome. Come on, Jamey, bath time."

After he'd cleared the dishes, he took a quick look through the open door of the bathroom and said good-night to them both. Ty was done, physically finished, and worried his exhaustion might get him blabbing again. He did not want a quiet moment alone with her once the baby was in bed.

Jamey, wet and pink, was now as covered with bub-bles as he had been with chicken potpie. He leaned for-ward, arms upstretched, making loud smacking noises.

"He wants a kiss."

"He might as well learn now that what he wants and what he gets are two different things."

"Did you learn that from the ranch hands?" she shot back at him.

"Yeah. I did. The cowboy way. And it has stood me in good stead, too."

"I can clearly see you radiate happiness," she said sweetly.

He gave her a sour look and went into his bedroom, away from *that* look in her eyes, knowing and sympathetic. Well, he had no one to blame but himself, blabbing his life history to her.

From behind his closed bedroom door, Ty slipped off his jeans and rolled into bed. He could hear the bath noises. Someone was obviously *radiating* happiness.

The baby's bath time was imbued with the same level of enthusiasm and joy as eating had been. There was gleeful chortles, splashing, motorboat noises, gurgles, clapping and games.

Ty tried putting his pillow over his head.

All it did was muffle the happiness that had invaded his house.

And then the invaders were in the bedroom beside his. Ty had moved Amy's suitcase off his bed and in there. He only had two bedrooms, so she was going to have to share the space she had set up for the baby. There was a twin bed, she had a playpen set up with a little nest of pale blue blankets and stuffed toys in its confines for the baby to sleep in.

Ty realized how thin the walls were. He gave up on the pillow. She didn't ever have to know he was eavesdropping on story time.

She read three stories, and Ty found himself hanging on every word. He recognized the stories, ones he had begged the kindergarten teacher to lend him, in love with stories from the first encounter. That teacher had been a kind woman, and lent the little motherless boy all the books he could haul home.

He had shown his father the books hopefully, but his dad had looked baffled by them. He'd flipped through them impatiently, looking at the pictures of little creatures dressed in human clothes and living in human houses with amazed dismay. Then he'd shoved the precious books back at Ty.

"I don't have time for make-believe," he'd said gruffly.

And so, carefully, greedily, looking at pictures and sounding out the words to *Curious George* and others by himself in his bed at night, long after his exhausted father had gone to sleep, he would read by flashlight.

Only years later did Ty figure out his father's reading skills were only rudimentary. His father had always known Halliday Creek Ranch would be his life, just as it had been his father's before that. He had not seen a use for education, and school had been a painful experience for him, one he could not wait to leave behind.

Now, listening to the stories, Ty wondered if his father had *wanted* to read to him. He dismissed the thought as quickly as it came.

Amy finished the bedtime stories with a tale Ty had not heard, called *Love You Forever,* and Ty felt the emotionally evocative words pull on someplace in him like a gathering storm.

He could hear her putting the baby in the playpen, imagined her covering him with a blanket. There was not a single protest.

And then he knew why.

She had saved the best for last.

She began to sing Jamey lullabies. Her voice was clear and true, shining like stars coming out in an evening sky.

And suddenly Ty's heart was heavy, and his eyes were heavy, and her soft voice was soaring in his ears. A yearning was sitting on his chest like a weight. It was for a wish unrealized. It was for all the things that had never been.

And that he had long since accepted would never be.

He slept when the songs were done, instantly and deeply, the sleep of an exhausted man.

When he awoke in the morning, he was aware of two things. First, it had snowed through the night, and probably hard. The house had that quiet to it, outside sounds of cattle and birds and horses muffled by a layer of snow on the ground and on the roof.

Second, he was intensely and instantly aware he was not in the house by himself. He was not sure why that awareness was so sharp. The child and the woman were making no sound, almost certainly still asleep in these predawn hours that he habitually woke in.

So, how did he know? The smells from last night's dinner, the chicken potpie scorched on the burner and the baby's bath lingering in the air?

No, those smells seemed to be gone, replaced by more tempting ones. Ty was sure he could faintly smell popcorn, and something else. Surely she hadn't got to baking after she'd put the baby to bed?

But more than smells, he knew it was being a man alone that had made him sensitive to the presence of others in his house. He could feel it tickling along his skin, almost as if the notes from her song had left something shivering in the air long after her voice had died away and both he and the baby had slept.

Ty rose quickly, dressed quietly and went on silent feet from his room.

The house was still, as he had known it would be, the guest room door slightly ajar.

He tiptoed through to the kitchen, put on coffee. He would take a travel mug with him, go outside and do chores without awakening his visitors. When he got back they would be up, and he could help her pack her stuff in her little car and wave at her as she went down the driveway.

She'd probably ask for an email address so she could keep in touch. And he didn't have one, so that would be the end of that.

He turned to the back porch, but a flicker of light drew his attention to the living room.

He froze, stared, moved forward.

Last night, when he had gone to bed, the tree had been at the same stage as when he had walked in the evening before. The lights had been on it, but nothing else.

Now, as if Santa's elves had appeared in the night, it had been transformed into a glorious thing. The lights had been left plugged in and winked with bright cheer. The star shone like a beacon from the top of it.

Astoundingly, the tree had been completely decorated.

Ty could barely see the offensive artificial branches there was so much stuff on the tree. He was sure those few scant boxes of decorations could not have filled the branches like this.

Almost against his will, he was drawn closer.

He had smelled popcorn. Strings of it were looped around the tree. And he *had* smelled baking. Because she had made up for the lack of ornaments by hanging cookies. He stepped closer again. The cookies were shaped like round ornaments, and like trees, and like Christmas parcels, all decorated with different colors of icing and sprinkles of candy.

It occurred to Ty that Amy must have arrived with all the things needed to make such intricate cookies stuffed into her little car, intent on making the perfect Christmas for her little boy.

And then, sometime yesterday, her intention had shifted.

She hadn't done this for Jamey.

They were leaving. They were leaving today.

No, she must have been up half the night doing this for him. Why? Ty thought he had made it clear that he did not invest in the sentiment of it all.

And that was probably why. She had been driven to show him what he was missing.

*Great. He had managed to invoke her pity.*

He tried to harden his heart to it, but it didn't work. Ty was shocked by how the gift of it wiggled by his customary cynicism, and made him feel a deep sense of humility.

Ty reached out, pulled one of the cookies off the tree, bit into it. It was delicious. He allowed a small smile. Perfect for him. An edible tree.

The chores needed doing, and he turned to leave all this magic behind him. He needed space around him— his space—to clear his head. And then he saw her.

Amy Mitchell was not in the guest room. She had fallen asleep in the big easy chair, curled up, her legs underneath her, her chin down on her neck. Her curls were flat in places and standing straight up in others. Her shirt was gaping open at the throat. The book he'd been reading and had left on a side table was spread out, open across her chest.

Had his choice of books told her something about him? He'd never been to university, but last year he had come across a reading list and was making his way through it. He moved Homer's *The Iliad* gently from her breast.

There was a blanket in a basket beside the chair and he hesitated. And then he took it and unfolded it, tucked it around her with a tenderness that astounded him. He fought off an impulse to touch those crazy curls.

He was glad she would be gone soon.

There was nothing in him that knew anything about being with a woman like this. She had seen his world was a hard place, with no soft edges, and made him the gift of the tree. Trying to show him something, or save him from something.

It didn't really matter which, because there was nothing in him that knew about the sensitivity and softness that would be required to appreciate a woman like this.

She represented everything he could not have.

And everything he had convinced himself he did not want, until he had heard her voice singing to the baby last night, woken up to the remarkably gentle gift of the tree. And he suspected that was her intention.

To let him have a glimpse at a softer world. To make him know he was missing something.

He turned his back on her swiftly. The thing about what she was offering him—once a man tasted that, he could start craving it. Craving was weakness.

He yanked on his boots, hat and coat, out of sorts now as he went out the back door. There he paused, stunned by what he saw. He had known from the muffled sounds this morning that it had snowed.

Nothing could have prepared him for how much.

The accumulated snow, when he stepped off his back stair, was nearly at his knee. In his lifetime, he had not seen so much snow in one dump. And the dump wasn't over. Though no snow was falling at the moment, the sky was leaden, the mountains obscured by thick, ominous cloud. He sniffed the air and could smell the threat. There was more snow coming.

He plowed a path with his boots, around the side of his house, to the front. He surveyed his driveway, though he had already known what he would see.

Her car was somewhere under a mound of snow that was precisely the same size and shape as an igloo.

It would take a hard day of plowing with his tractor to make his driveway reappear from under a stretch of snow that rolled clear to the mountains. And with more snow coming, was there any point in tackling that task?

Besides, beyond his driveway would the roads be open? Possibly. He would be able to turn on the radio and find out.

But what if the roads were open? A big truck with four-wheel drive and a driver with more guts than brains could get through on them.

But Ty felt as if it would border on criminal to allow her and the baby to leave in these conditions.

These conditions. The reality hit him.

*Snowed in.*

Ty remembered "snow" days from when he was a kid. Days the school bus couldn't get through on the roads. And since then, every few years there would be a day or two when he didn't get to the driveway with the plow and was stuck on the place.

It was never a big deal. He always had a freezer full of beef, a pantry stocked with tinned goods.

But now he had unexpected guests. And if felt like a very big deal, indeed. How long was she going to be here?

With a sinking heart, he realized it was going to be another day, at the very least.

He reminded himself the native people, so in tune with this land and the larger picture, would say just to make the best of it.

But when he thought of her singing to the baby, and that tree in his house, her gentle gift to him, and when he thought of how he felt tucking the blanket around her, he knew how easy it would be to feel attached to them.

That had really been his unspoken motto through much of his life: No Attachments.

He refused even to own a dog, the most pragmatic of men, he didn't see a cute little puppy. He saw how it was going to end.

Amy was stuck here. He was stuck with her. It was his job now to make sure they all got out of it with no one getting hurt.

He had to be indifferent to her. He had to. Not for his sake, but for hers. A long time ago, when he'd run wild on the rodeo circuit, a girl had told him, tearfully,

*Cowboy, you are the kind of guy who breaks hearts. Because you don't have one.*

So he just had to be himself, which was a heartless bastard. That shouldn't be too difficult for him. When he was able to get the driveway clear, Amy Mitchell would be so glad to get gone, that little car would go down the road as if it had been shot from a catapult.

As he was finishing up his chores, the snow had started again. The flakes were huge and wet, nearly obliterating his house from his view.

He came in the back door, knowing he had to tell her the bad news quick and get it over with. He glanced up from the porch and saw Amy sitting at the kitchen table. She looked pale, and her eyes smarted with tears.

At first he thought she must have already figured out she wasn't going anywhere. But then something about her stillness, and the look on her face, made him take the stairs two at time.

The frying pan was on the stove, turned off, half-cooked bacon in it.

"What happened?"

Mutely, she held one hand toward him, the fingers of her other hand circling a wrist that was as tiny, her bones as fragile as a sparrow's.

"I—I—I never used that kind of pan before. I didn't realize the handle would get so hot."

"What the—" he glanced at the hundred-year-old cast-iron frying pan, and then looked at her hand.

Across the palm was a welt, angry-looking and puckered, the imprint of the pan handle scorched into her skin like a brand.

He went on his knees in front of her, but when he

reached out to take her hand, to get a better look, she yanked it away.

"I might have to go to the hospital," she said, her effort at bravery diminished somewhat by the fact her whole body was trembling.

"Let me look."

She didn't want to trust him. Smart girl. But there was no one else, and so he captured her hand, held it firm, studied the burn. Bad, but not hospital bad, which given the condition of the roads was a good thing.

"Stupid of me," she said in a wooden voice.

He looked up from her hand.

"Just like coming here by accident. Dumb. It's what they all expect, and they're all right."

It occurred to him it wasn't because she hadn't trusted him that she hadn't wanted to show him her hand.

It was because she was afraid of being judged. Found stupid.

For a guy who didn't have a heart, he was surprised by where he felt that.

"Who?" he said quietly.

And then she was crying, big fat tears slithering down her cheeks.

"Everybody. My husband, his parents, my parents. Everybody treats me like I can't ever do anything right. Can't be trusted to make good decisions."

Considering how he had dreaded the thought of her crying when it had almost happened yesterday, considering he had a fully formulated plan that had *heartless bastard* at its core, Ty surprised himself by not bolting for the door.

Instead, inwardly, calmly, he acknowledged it would take a stronger man than he was to be indifferent to her.

Her palm still lay across his hand. He lifted it to his lips and blew gently on the burn. She went very still, and he looked up at her.

"Hey," he said, "it's going to be okay."

"It hurts so bad."

He wasn't quite sure if she meant the burn, or everyone's low expectations of her. He remembered seeing something in her face when she had said she was a widow, a torment of some kind. He'd thought it was because of her loss. Now he wondered if it wasn't a loss of a different sort instead.

"I'll fix it."

And he wasn't quite sure what he meant by that, either. The burn, or the wounded place in her that was so much deeper than the burn.

The burn would be easy.

And surely Ty had enough self-knowledge to know he could not be trusted with the other?

And then, even though his jacket was cold and wet with melting flakes of snow, she put her arms around his neck.

He felt her uninjured hand, warm and soft, trace the coldness of the exposed skin on the back of his neck. The other she held away from him. She leaned forward and put her forehead against his, drew in a deep trembling breath. He stiffened.

For a moment he froze, uncertain what to do with all this pain and all this trust.

And then the certainty came. As naturally as breathing, he put his arms around her and pulled her close into him, so close that he could feel her heart beating against the oilskin of the jacket. So close that her tears slithered down his neck along with melting snow.

And he held her, and then, something in him surrendered. He did what he realized he had wanted to do since the moment he had first seen her peeking at him from behind his tree.

He ran his fingers through her hair, and felt the tangles dissolve under his touch. She pulled back from him slightly, looked him in the face, and then leaned forward and kissed him lightly on his lips.

"Thank you," she said huskily.

For what? All he'd managed to do, so far, was break his vow to himself to keep his distance, to keep them all safe from the treachery of attachment.

He reeled back from her, scrambled to his feet. She looked as though she was going to cry even harder, of course. She was probably realizing she'd just done something *really* dumb.

He resisted the urge to wipe his lips. It wouldn't do what he wanted anyway. It wouldn't remove the sweet, clean taste of her.

That was branded on his mind as surely as the frying pan had left a mark on her delicate skin.

In the guest bedroom, the baby started to cry. If someone had told him yesterday he would welcome a baby crying, Ty would have scoffed.

But now it was just the diversion from all this intensity that he needed.

"I'll get him," he said.

"No, I can—"

"No, you can't." He sounded really stern and cold,

which was a good thing. Rebuilding his fences. "I don't want you to touch anything until I've got a dressing on the burn. When you are in a remote location like this, the wound generally isn't the problem. It's infection. Think of *Lonesome Dove*."

*Yeah, he ordered himself, think of* Lonesome Dove. *Not her lips.*

"Lonesome Dove?"

"On my top twenty list of good books." Why had he said that? She did not need to know he had a top twenty list. She did not need to know one more thing about him! He was pretty sure that's how attachments were formed, these little bits of information knitting together into a chain.

Kissing didn't help, either.

"I only have the vaguest notion what you are talking about." Was she staring at his lips? With *longing?*

*Buck up, cowboy.*

"It's not the arrow that finishes the main character, it's infection. I'll get the baby."

"Yesterday, you didn't even want to pick him up!" she reminded him. "You could barely give him a pat on the head."

"Well, yesterday I didn't have to. Today, I do."

Ty left her, shrugged off his coat and boots in the porch, and then went to the bedroom door and looked in at the baby.

Jamey had hauled himself up on the rails of the playpen, and was jumping up and down, howling his outrage at being imprisoned.

"Hey, that's enough out of you."

Jamey stopped jumping up and down and stopped

howling. He smiled, and made a little goo-goo sound, instantly charming.

"Papa Odam," he declared. His arms shot out. "Up."

Ty went in. This was how old he had been when his mother had walked out the door and scarcely looked back. Or at least that was what he had believed. Until the letters.

Is this what his father had felt that day?

Terrified? As if he'd been left in charge of something breakable and didn't have a clue what to do?

"Up." It wasn't a request, the charm dissolving. It was a command.

"Are you always so bossy?" he said to the baby.

Ty felt a nudge of sympathy for his dad, just like he had felt last night when he'd heard Amy reading stories and wondered if his dad had wanted to read to him.

Funny that he would feel sympathy when the letters had resurfaced. Rationally, that should make him angry all over again.

He thought of Amy singing last night, and seeing the tree, and putting the blanket on her this morning. He thought of her tears and his hands in her hair. He thought of the exquisite softness of her lips taking his.

"Up!"

"All right, already."

Taking a deep breath, he leaned over and picked up the baby.

It was not a tender moment. The baby stank to high heaven.

And yet as that stinky baby snuggled into him, Ty was aware for the first time that that long ago girl who had accused him of not having a heart, had not been right after all.

Because he did have a heart. He could feel it beating as Jamey pressed deeper against him, sighed happily, as if it were a homecoming.

It was that he had built walls around it, an impenetrable fortress.

It was obviously Amy's fault, even before the complication of her lips touching his, that the walls were being compromised, the fortress being threatened. Softness was flowing through the barriers like water onto parched earth. Allowing that softness in was why, without warning, he felt sympathy for a man he had barely spoken to for years.

And he didn't know how, in the end, any of this could possibly be a good thing.

# CHAPTER FOUR

*WHAT had she done?*

Amy sank back in her chair, listened to the gruff masculine melody of Ty talking to Jamey down the hallway in the guest bedroom.

She had kissed him. She had kissed Ty Halliday. That's what she had done. There were excuses of course: the pain of the burn had knocked down her normal quota of reserve. Still, she waited for regret to swim around her like a shark sensing blood. Giving in to the temptation to taste his lips was just more evidence of her stupidity.

But the regret did not come.

How could she regret that? Taking his lips in hers had felt like a conscious decision, entirely empowering. And she could still feel the shiver of pure sensation. She thought she might remember it as long as she lived.

She was leaving, anyway. As soon as the roads were passable, she would be gone. So what did it matter that, when he had put his arms around her, she had felt for the first time in a long, long time as if she had fallen and there had been a net waiting to catch her?

That's what the kiss had been about.

Pure gratitude.

Instead of agreeing with her that she had indeed been stupid about burning herself, about winding up here when she needed to be somewhere else, his voice had been deep and calm and reassuring.

*Hey, it's going to be okay.*

Instead of pointing out to her all the different ways she could have avoided the situation, and all the trouble she had caused, he had just said, simply, *I'll fix it.*

If something other than gratitude had shivered to life in that brief second when her lips had touched his and her world had tilted crazily, so what? Again, she was leaving. Whatever else had been there—some primal awareness, some wrenching hunger—would have no opportunity to blossom to life.

Whatever *that* had been, he had felt it, too. Right down to the toes of his wet cowboy boots. He'd pulled away from her as if he'd got a jolt form a cattle prod.

Amy chided herself. She should have the decency at least to be embarrassed. But she did not feel embarrassed.

She felt, again, oddly and delightfully empowered. That big, self-assured cowboy was just a little bit afraid of what had happened between them. He had built a world where he had absolute control, and it could be nothing but a good thing for that attitude to be challenged now and then!

Ty came back into the kitchen with Jamey. The baby looked ridiculously happy to find himself in Ty's arms.

There was something terrifyingly beautiful about seeing a tiny child in the arms of such a man.

It was a study in contrasts. The man's skin etched by sun and wind and a hint of rough, dark whisker, the baby's skin as tender as the fuzzy inside of a creamy rose petal. The man had easy certainty in his own rugged strength, the baby was like a melting puddle of skin and bone. The man's eyes held shadows, the baby's innocence. The man's mouth was a stern line of cynicism, the baby's a curve of pure joy.

And of course, the man was totally self-reliant, the baby totally the opposite. And in this moment, Ty had assumed the mantle of responsibility for the baby's reliance.

It surprised her that, given his reluctance to hold the baby yesterday, Ty looked relatively comfortable with his little charge. He dodged the pudgy finger trying to insert itself in his nose with the ease and grace of a bullfighter who had done it all a thousand times.

Then Amy caught a whiff of her charming offspring. She was amazed that Ty had him in the crook of his arm, nestled against his chest, that Jamey wasn't being held at arm's length like a bomb about to go off.

"I don't expect you to deal with *that,*" she said.

"Oh, really?" He raised that dark slash of a brow at her. "Who do you expect to deal with it?"

That silenced her. Who did she expect to deal with it? Her hand felt as if it was on fire. It actually hurt so bad that she felt nauseous. She was not sure she could do a one-handed diaper change, even if she could fight through the haze of physical pain. And then there *was* the question of infection.

Ty set Jamey down on the baby blanket, still spread out on the kitchen floor. "Where's his stuff? You'll have to give me step-by-step instructions."

She directed Ty to the diaper bag, watched him set it

down on the floor and get down on his knees between the baby and the bag.

"Prepare yourself," she said. "This is not going to be pretty."

Ty leveled a look at her. "Lady, I've been up to my knees in all kinds of crap since I was old enough to walk. I've watched animals being born, and I've watched them die. And I've seen plenty of stuff in between that wasn't anything close to pretty. So if you think there's anything about what's about to happen that would faze me, you're about as wrong as you can get."

"I'm just saying men aren't good at this."

"Look, there are things a man *wants* to be good at."

Did his eyes actually linger on her lips as he said that before he turned his attention to the diaper bag?

"In my world," he informed her, digging through the bag, "a man wants to be good at throwing a rope. He wants to be good at riding anything that has four legs. He wants to be good at turning a green colt into a reliable cow horse."

His words were drawing rather enticing pictures in her mind.

"He wants to be good at starting a fire with no matches and wet wood. He wants to be good with his fists if he's backed into a corner and there is no other way out. He wants to be good at tying a fly that will call a trout out of a brook."

"This—" he gestured at her son, lying down, legs flaying the air and releasing clouds of odor "—is not something any man aspires to be good at. The question is, can he get the job done?"

"I may have stated it wrong. I simply meant it's not something men do well."

"Are you going to be grading me on this?"

Suddenly, Amy *needed* to share it, as if it was a secret burden she had carried alone for too long. She suddenly needed another person's perspective.

"My late husband, Edwin, changed Jamey's diaper twice. Twice. Both times it was a production. Clothes peg on the nose, gagging, brown blotches on the walls, the floor, the baby and his Hugo Boss shirt. The diaper was finally on inside out and backward to the declaration of 'good enough.'"

Edwin's efforts, she remembered, had always been good enough. Hers, not so much. She had asked him to do less and less. Amy had hoped for something else. In her marriage. And especially with the baby. Shared trials. Magical moments. Much laughter.

The pain of the remembered disappointment felt nearly as bad as the pain in her hand.

Ty glanced at her sharply, as if he was seeing something she had not intended for him to see.

"Twice?" he said. "And the baby was three months old when he died?"

She nodded.

"And he managed to be put out both times?"

She nodded again. "But he was a CEO of a corporation," she said. "Strictly white collar."

"I got that at the Hugo Boss part," he said drily. "And you know what? His perception of his own importance is a damn poor excuse."

She had wanted this perspective. Needed desperately

to know it wasn't her, expecting too much, being unreasonably demanding.

But now that she had it, she felt a guilty need to defend her husband.

"He was a busy, important man. I'm afraid he had better things to do than change a diaper."

She remembered asking Edwin to do it. Insisting. Getting *that* look. All she had wanted was for him to empathize with her life. She had wanted him to be more hands-on with the baby. She had wanted him to appreciate what she did every day. Maybe she wasn't even sure what she had wanted.

But whatever it was, Edwin's annoyed look down at his shirt, and his *Are you happy now?* had not been it.

Ty rocked back on his heels and looked at her hard. She felt as if every lonely night she had spent in her marriage was visible for him to see.

"You know what?" he said, his voice a growl of pure disgust, "I'm beginning to really dislike Edwin."

Her sense of guilt deepened. Why had she brought this up? "He was not a bad person because he didn't like changing diapers," she said. "That would make a huge percentage of the world's population bad people."

"It's not about the diapers," he said quietly. "It's about what you said earlier, too. As if you having an accident and burning your hand made you stupid. It's about him making you feel like you were less than him."

She was stunned by that. Her relationship with Edwin had never been defined quite so succinctly.

She had been so alone with her feeling of deficiency, questioning herself.

"He's dead," she reminded Ty primly, the only defense left that she could think of.

"Yeah, well, that doesn't automatically elevate him to sainthood."

She thought of the shrine being built in his parents' living room. In conversation, the new and improved version of Edwin was what her in-laws insisted on remembering and immortalizing.

And her guilt intensified at how relieved she was that someone—anyone—could see something else.

She changed the subject abruptly, feeling as if she was going to throw herself at him all over again. It was just wrong to be feeling this much kinship over a diaper change, of all things.

He rummaged through the bag, held up a diaper for her inspection. At her nod, he said, "Check."

He laid out her whole checklist of items in a neat line on the blanket: baby wipes, petroleum jelly, baby powder and the diaper.

"Isn't that how soldiers take apart weapons?" she asked.

"Precisely," he said, pleased by the analogy.

"Okay. Now you lay him down and take off his pajamas. They're Onesies—

"Whatsies?"

"Onesies, one-piece jumpers, so you undo all the snaps down the front and right down his leg and slip him out."

"Like slipping a banana out of a peel," he said. "It's even yellow."

"Well, yes, kind of—"

"Except bananas don't leak, uh, brown blotches." He grimaced, but there was no gagging, no drama.

In one swift movement he had plump limbs out of the pajamas, and had them off. In another move, he slipped off the soiled diaper. He dispensed with both items with nary a flinch.

Jamey kicked wildly, and Ty caught the little feet easily in one hand.

"Hey," he warned, "cut it out." But it was a mild warning. He also did not flinch from cleaning Jamey up. He was methodical and thorough, and as he had promised, unfazed by the task. The minefield of petroleum jelly and diaper tabs did not claim him as a victim.

In fact, in short order, the baby was in a new diaper, gurgling happily and kicking his legs.

Ty picked up the messy items and disappeared. The diaper went out the back door, and then she heard him washing his hands in the bathroom.

When he came back, he had a new Onesies and had snitched one of the cookies off the tree. He slipped the baby into the new jammies, and handed the cookie to him.

"That should keep him busy while I look at your hand. I put the banana peel in the sink to soak the brown blotches until we have time to run a load of laundry."

She wasn't running a load of laundry. She was *leaving*. The need to go was feeling increasingly urgent.

Because watching him, and the apparent ease with which he adapted to what life threw at him—a baby and a woman invading his bachelor cave and the woman now nearly completely incapacitated—she felt sudden awareness of the tall self-assured cowboy shiver up her spine.

As he came and sat in the chair opposite her, and then pulled it so close their knees were touching, she was totally aware of Ty Halliday as pure man.

"Let me see your hand again."

This time she just gave it to him willingly, watched as he took it and steadied it on his own knee. He bent his head over it, and she felt a deep thrill at his physical closeness. His scent filled her world—clean, mysterious, masculine. The overhead kitchen light danced in the rich, pure gold of his hair.

His touch was exquisite.

After inspecting the damage thoroughly, he surrendered her hand back to her and got up. She followed him with her eyes as he reached up above his fridge and retrieved a first-aid kit.

Amy felt as if she was in a lovely altered state of awareness where she could appreciate the broadness of his shoulders, the narrowness of his hips, the slight swell of his rear under the snug fit of his jeans, the impossible length of his legs.

He turned back to her, his expression one of complete calm and utter confidence.

He knew what to do. And he was not the least bit afraid or hesitant to do it.

It struck her, as he moved back toward her, his grace and strength unconscious, that Ty had all the ingredients that had made men men since the beginning of time.

As he sat back down, she saw the intensity of his focus in the amazing sapphire of his eyes. She saw him as a warrior, a hunter, a protector, an explorer, a cowboy and a king.

Obviously, changing diapers and dressing wounds had not been in his plan for the day.

But Ty Halliday had no whine in him. No complaint.

What she saw was a stoic acceptance of what it meant to be a man, an unconscious confidence in his ability to rise to any occasion and do what needed to be done, whether that was putting in long hours doing rugged ranch work, or whether it was nursing something—or someone—injured.

The diaper had not been pretty. Neither was her wound.

And yet he did not shirk from either one. She suspected there was very little he would not face head-on.

She was not sure why, but that simple competence left her almost breathless with awe, tingling with a physical awareness of him, and of the space he was taking up in her world.

On the kitchen table that was beside them he again laid things out with the precision of a solider taking apart a familiar weapon. From the first-aid kit he removed individually packaged disinfectant wipes, antibiotic ointment, gauze pads, gauze wrap, scissors, tiny metal clips.

He surveyed the lineup of materials, remembered something, got up and reached into the cabinet above the fridge again. He came back with one more thing.

Amy gasped when he set it down, her awareness of his considerable masculine charm competing with this latest item. At the very end of his line of first-aid items, he had added a very large needle, attached to an even larger syringe.

"What's that for?" she asked.

"Penicillin. Don't worry about it." He picked up her hand, cradled it in his. With his other hand and his teeth, he opened a package and removed an antiseptic wipe from it.

She barely registered that. She was not sure she had ever seen such a large needle. She gulped. "You can't just give a person a needle, you know."

He swabbed the burn.

"You can't?" he asked, unconcerned. She watched him as he tore open a second antiseptic wipe with his teeth and cleaned the whole area again. She glanced back at the needle.

"You have to be a doctor."

"I didn't know that." He tossed aside the used wipes, opened the tube of ointment, squeezed some out onto the palm of her hand.

Gently, he smoothed the ointment over the burn.

At any other time, she might have appreciated the gentle certainty of his touch. But she couldn't seem to take her eyes off that needle, and its place in the lineup.

"Or at least a nurse."

"I've given thousands of needles." He inspected her hand, and then satisfied, covered the burn with a gauze pad, item number three. The needle and syringe were item number seven and he was making his way steadily toward them.

"Thousands?" she asked with jittery skepticism.

"Literally. Thousands. To cows and horses, but I'm pretty sure the technique is the same. Or similar."

He took the roll of gauze, item number four, and began to unwind it firmly around the pad in the palm of her hand.

"It isn't," she told him. "It's not the same technique. It's not even similar."

"How do you know? How many horses have you given needles to?" He was making a neat figure eight over her burned palm, around her thumb and up her wrist. He went around and around, his movements smooth, sure, mesmerizing.

"Well, none. I haven't actually ever given a needle to anything. But it just makes sense that giving one to a person and an animal are totally different things."

She heard a certain shrill nervousness in her voice.

In contrast, his was low and calm. "Don't worry, Amy, I'm not going to hurt you."

"On purpose," she said. "You might by accident."

He glanced up at her sharply. She had a woozy sense of not being at all sure they were still talking about the needle.

"I'll try not to."

No promises, she noticed.

He picked up the scissors, item number five, cut the gauze wrap. She glanced over at the table. He was nearly done.

He picked up the little metal clips, item number six, pulled the end of the gauze wrap firm on top of her wrist and inserted the teeth of the clips into the thickest place on the gauze. He gave his handiwork a satisfied pat.

"You can't just give a person penicillin," she said, staring at what remained in his neat lineup on the table—number seven, the syringe and needle. "You need a prescription for it!"

"Okay."

She eyed him suspiciously. He seemed to acquiesce

just a little too easily. She watched narrowly as he methodically repacked the first aid kit. He picked it up, and almost as an afterthought, picked up the huge needle and syringe. He stowed them all back in the cupboard above the fridge.

"Oh!" she said, and let out a huge breath of relief. "You never planned on using the needle! You scared me on purpose."

"Dressing a burn hurts like hell. I prefer to think of it as a distraction," he said, and then he smiled.

His smile was absolutely devastating. It took him from stern and formidable to boyishly charming in a blink.

She looked down at her hand. He had distracted her on purpose, and she honestly didn't know if she was grateful or annoyed by how gullible she was, but the smile made it impossible to be annoyed with him no matter how annoyed she was at herself.

And she realized the syringe and needle had indeed been a distraction. But that distraction had existed in the background. In the foreground had been the exquisiteness of his touch, his strength so tempered by gentleness, that pleasure and pain had become merged into a third sensation altogether.

And that third sensation scorched through her, more powerfully than the burn.

It was desire.

She wanted to kiss him again. Harder this time. Longer.

She had to get away from here. She was just in the baby stages of getting her life back in order. This was no time for kissing and all the complications that kissing could bring.

She'd known this man less than twenty-four hours. What was she thinking? The truth? She wasn't thinking at all. She was falling under some kind of spell, an enchantment that had been deepened by tasting him, and then by the drugging sensuality of his easy smile.

He had a tea towel in his hand now. "Sorry. I don't have a real sling. I'll improvise with this."

"I don't need a sling!" Imagine how close to her he'd have to get to put that on!

"It'll be better if we immobilize your hand. If we don't, you'll be surprised by how often you want to use it. You could just try it for today."

"But I won't be able to drive if my arm is in a sling."

His gaze slid away from her before he turned back, opened his palm and held out two white pills.

"You generally need a prescription for these, too. We're a long way from an emergency ward here. We take some liberties."

"I really won't be able to drive if I take those." *Or,* she added to herself, *keep my head about me.*

"No, you won't."

"Then I'd better not."

"Ah, well, there's something I have to tell you. The driveway isn't passable. I'm going to turn on the radio and see what the roads are like, not that it really matters if you can't get out of the driveway." He glanced to the window. "Don't get your hopes up. It's snowing again."

Her eyes drifted to the window. Snowing again was an understatement. The window looked as if it had been washed with white paint, the snow beyond it was so thick light could barely penetrate. She felt panic surge in her.

This terrible wave of affection had been building in her since he had changed Jamey. Shamefully, it had grown even more when he'd said he disliked her husband.

That sensation of someone having her back had deepened the emotion she was feeling for him.

And now that he had dressed her hand so gently, with such skill, distracting her from the pain, she felt a terrible danger from the desire that was beating like a steady pulse at the core of her being.

"You can't possibly mean I can't get out of here!" She knew she was saying it like it was his fault. She knew it wasn't.

His silence was answer.

"But for how long?" she asked, her voice shrill with desperation.

"It won't be long," he said in a tone one might use trying to divert a small child from having a temper tantrum. She was done with his diversions.

"That isn't a real answer."

"I don't have a crystal ball. I don't have a real answer."

"If you were going to guess?" she pressed him.

He hesitated. "I'd say tomorrow. If it stops snowing in the next hour or so I can get the driveway plowed by then. I'll put on the radio and get the weather forecast."

"I'm trapped," she whispered.

"Well, not limb-in-leg-hold-trap trapped, but not-going-anywhere-today trapped." He sounded just a little tongue-in-cheek. He clearly did not understand the gravity of this situation!

Her new life, her new plan for herself was being threatened by him. It was being threatened and she had been here less than twenty-four hours. She'd kissed a man she barely knew and wanted to do it again.

What kind of mess would she be in forty-eight hours from now?

Maybe she would be ripping off his clothes and chasing him around the kitchen. Not that she was that type.

Good heavens, she had never been that type.

But she was well aware that the "type" she had been—pleasing other people in the hope they would play their role in her fantasy of the perfect home and family—had not brought her one iota of happiness. Not one.

That realization left her wide-open to being pulled down the road of temptation.

"But there could be an emergency!" she said, knowing there had to be a way out of here if the stakes were high enough.

"An emergency? What kind of emergency?"

The thought that there might be an emergency of the magnitude that he could not handle seemed to take him totally by surprise.

"Like a medical emergency. Not a little burn, either. What if something happens to Jamey? What if he gets sick and has a temperature of one hundred and three? What if he fell down the steps and broke his neck?"

Ty rocked back on his heels and regarded her with just a trace of exasperation. He held out the white pills. "If you don't take these, I think I might," he said, his tone dry.

"You have to think of the possibilities!"

"No, I don't. There are millions of possibilities. That is way more thinking than I care to do. The phone is working. The power is on. We have heat and food. We could probably get a helicopter in if a real emergency happened. It won't."

"How can you know that?" She was slightly mollified that they could get a helicopter in, even as she was aware the real danger she needed to escape was something else entirely.

He shrugged. "I just know."

And, despite herself, she believed him. He knew his world inside out and backward. He trusted himself in it and that made her, however reluctantly, trust him, too. She was the wild card in all this, not him. Imagine her, Amy Mitchell, being a wild card.

Still, taking the pills seemed like it would threaten her control just a little too completely, so she pushed them aside just as the phone rang.

He got up and got it. He listened for a moment, and then without a word, brought her the receiver. The line of his mouth was turned downward, and he raised an eyebrow at her.

How could it be for her?

Puzzled, she took it.

"Amy, what is going on? Are you with a man?"

Ah. The miracles of modern technology. Yesterday, when her cell phone had not worked, she had called from here. The number must have come up on her mother-in-law, Cynthia's, caller ID unit.

"Hello, Cynthia. Please calm down, everything is fine."

"What do you mean everything is fine! And do not tell me to calm down in that snotty tone of voice, young lady. You have my grandson and you are with a man. Who is that man?"

Somehow, everything Amy was running from was in that strident tone. Judgment. Lack of trust. Disapproval.

"He's—" Amy glanced at him. The explanation seemed complicated. And would confirm every single thing Cynthia already thought. Amy really wasn't ready to admit she had lost her way yet, especially not to her supercritical, always ready to pounce mother-in-law. If towels not folded correctly could bring that pinched look of pained forbearance, how much worse was this going to be?

Amy took a deep breath and turned away from Ty so she didn't have to see his reaction to what she was about to say. "I'm having trouble with the laundry. He's the washer repairman."

"How come the washer repairman is answering the phone?" Cynthia asked, her voice shrill and full of suspicion.

"Uh, how come he answered the phone? Uh—" And suddenly, Ty was standing in front of her. He held out his hand.

It would be downright cowardly to give him the phone and let him handle her mother-in-law.

She looked into his eyes, saw the man she was trusting with her life and the life of her baby, and surrendered the phone.

He took it and winked at her. *Winked!*

"This is the washer repairman," he said, his voice

solemn. "We are having an emergency. Brown blotches. It's not a good time to talk."

And then he hung up the phone, crossed his arms and gazed at Amy.

"She's going to phone right back," Amy warned him.

The phone started to ring.

Ty reached behind Amy's back and pulled the plug from the wall.

There was so much he could say. But he didn't. And there was so much she could say, but she didn't, either.

She giggled. And then giggled again.

He smiled, and then he laughed. His laughter was possibly the most beautiful sound she had ever heard. It was rich and clean and without any kind of mockery in it. No reprimand about lying. No advice about how to handle her pushy mother-in-law.

The laughter flowed out of him, like water tumbling over rocks, and suddenly with absolutely no warning a sweet feeling of absolute freedom filled Amy.

For the first time since she had married Edwin, Amy did not feel trapped at all. She savored the irony of that. She was trapped, really, by all the snow.

"You know what, Amy?" Ty finally said, wiping at his eyes. "I think it's time to have some fun."

"No offense," she said, wiping at her eyes, too, "but you don't look like you know that much about having fun."

His eyes went to her lips and locked there. That slow smile played across the sinfully sensuous line of his mouth.

He moved very close to her. His lips were so close to her ear, she could feel the heat of his breath on her skin.

"I guess," he growled, "that would depend on how you defined fun."

# CHAPTER FIVE

Amy was staring at him, and Ty could tell she was actually holding her breath, waiting for him to suggest something really fun, and perhaps a little naughty, like maybe tasting each other's lips again.

And while that would definitely be fun, the repercussions of such foolishness—even allowing the thought into his brain for three or four red-hot seconds—seemed truly dangerous.

Besides, he could tell she was not that kind of girl. But he could also tell it probably wouldn't take much of a shove to move her in that direction.

She was impossibly uptight, and when a string was pulled that taut, it was the easiest thing in the world to break. Plus, he had sensed something in that kiss that had made him pull back sharply from it.

Hunger. Raw and powerful. Had it been all his? Or had there been plenty of hers, too?

So, no, tempting as it might have been to follow the road that had opened up when she had kissed him, he had something else in mind for fun. He wasn't taking the low road. For goodness' sake, she had decorated a Christmas tree for him. Having any kind of naughty fun with her would be like fooling around with one of Santa's elves.

No, with the baby looking on a PG rating would be the best thing for everyone.

"The most fun a person can ever have on this earth?" he asked her, adding to himself *at least in the wholesome category.*

"Yes?" she breathed.

"Playing with a horse."

"Oh." She definitely looked disappointed. There was a wildcat in her waiting to be unleashed, and Ty wasn't quite sure if he envied or pitied the man who was going to be the one to unleash that.

"I'm actually, er, terrified of horses."

"I kind of figured." He watched her fiddle nervously with the dressing around her hand.

"What?" Her head flew up. "How would you figure that?"

"Hmm, let's see. You're scared of your car getting stolen and your house being broken in to. You're petrified of needles. Being snowed in has opened a whole world of dreadful possibilities that you never even considered before. And you're terrified of whoever that was on the phone."

"My mother-in-law."

He wondered if she was still Amy's mother-in-law since the husband was dead, but decided now was not the time to debate the technicalities of it.

They were stuck here together.

What if taking the high road meant he could show her one small thing? She had given him that Christmas tree. What if he gave her something in return?

What if he could show her there was nothing to be afraid of?

Given how filled she was with terror, he saw it was something of a miracle that she had packed up that baby in the middle of winter and headed into the unknown.

A miracle, or one desperate last-ditch effort to save herself, to truly live.

But if she could not tame all that fear, he saw the outcome as being predictable. Just as a horse went back into a barn that was engulfed in flames, Amy would go right back to what was familiar, no matter how uncomfortable that was. And that voice on the phone, shrill and demanding, asking him who he was without even saying hello? That would be plenty uncomfortable.

Ty had told Amy he had no religion. But the truth was, you could not live in a place like this, so close to the formidable majesty of nature, without seeing the order of things, that life unfolded with reason, that sometimes the smallest things that appeared random at first ended up being connected to a larger picture.

Was there a possibility that Amy Mitchell had arrived on his doorstep, not by accident, but for a reason?

If that was true, he had to get beyond his petty need to protect his comfortable little world. Rise above his own fears.

But then his eyes went to her lips.

Starting with that one.

What if he could give her one small gift and help her find the fearless place in her? To do that, he was going to have to require more of himself, he was going to have to be more and do better.

"Come on. Get the baby ready."

"Maybe you should just go ahead without us. I can find things to do inside. It looks like a perfect day to bake bread."

She really didn't want to do this. At some level, she was figuring it out. Saying yes to him right now was going to put the way she lived her whole life at stake.

The incentive of fresh-baked bread nearly killed his new vow to be a better man.

"Are you using the promise of fresh-baked bread to distract me? Just like I used that needle to distract you? Because, really, fresh-baked bread to a bachelor is like offering water to someone lost in the desert."

Was that his life? Was he lost in the desert? He had never thought so before. This little bit of a thing was shaking up his life way beyond what her size should warrant!

He took in her look of relief.

"So," she said, "that's settled. I'll bake bread. You'll go play with horses. We'll both have fun, in our own ways."

"No."

"No?"

"I don't know that much about baking bread, but I'm pretty sure you need two hands to do it."

She looked, dismayed, at her wrapped hand.

"I told you we should put a sling on it as a reminder you are on the injured list. How about if you come play with me, and then I'll come play with you?"

"You'll help me bake bread?" Did she sound slightly skeptical?

"I've already demonstrated my great ability to catch

on with Mr. Splotchy over there. I hope baking bread is more fun than that."

"Well, it has to be more fun than that, but somehow I can't see you enjoying it. It's not very manly."

He laughed. "It would take more than helping to bake bread to threaten my masculinity. Do we have a deal?"

"I don't know."

That was an improvement over an out-and-out no.

"You know," he challenged her softly, "if you can learn to deal with a horse…"

She nodded.

"Your mother-in-law will be a piece of cake."

She went very still. She looked like a woman standing at the edge of a cliff, looking at the water below, deciding.

She jumped.

"Okay," she said, "I'm in."

And then she laughed again. And so did he. And she let him put her arm in a sling, which made him have to fight with his demons all over again. One kiss, right on the tender nape of that neck, where he was knotting the sling.

An hour later, he was congratulating himself because he had managed to fight off temptation and now they were all standing safely at the round corral, in his world.

Amy was wearing a bright toque with a fuzzy pompom on top and one of his jackets to accommodate the sling. She had one arm in the sleeve, the other tucked safely inside the jacket. The jacket, a plaid logger's coat came to his upper thigh when he wore it. On her it was past her knees.

It made her look adorable, small and lost, like an orphan standing on a street corner waiting for someone to take her home.

It had taken forever to get the baby into a snowsuit, but Jamey was in it now and looked like a bright blue marshmallow—felt like one, too—nestled into the curve of Ty's arm.

"So, this is Ben," Ty said as they all stood at the rail, looking at the horse in the round corral behind the barn.

The flakes were still dancing down around them, huge and unrelenting. Jamey kept bending over backward trying to catch snowflakes on his tongue, grumbling and yelling when they hit him in the eyes instead.

Ben was the horse Ty had ridden the day before. He was a good horse, young, part mustang, a red roan, with about the softest eyes Ty had ever seen on a horse.

"He's a two-year-old, which is basically a baby in horse years."

"He seems very large for a baby," Amy said cautiously. "His size alone makes me nervous."

"He'll be nervous if you're nervous. That's the secret about horses. They are looking to you for leadership. He *wants* you to lead him. We should go ahead and get in there with him."

"I don't know. He's so big. He could kill us."

"It's funny you should say that, because that's exactly what he's afraid of, too. Death by predator."

He was holding the baby, so when he went through the rails, she followed. Whether she would have if he didn't have the baby, Ty wasn't sure.

"The road's closed," she reminded him in a terrified whisper. "What if something happens?"

"Something is going to happen," he promised. "Pure magic. Stick close to me, walk as if you're a king."

"I'm the wrong sex to be a king," she muttered.

He was committed to wholesome. He didn't even want her using that word right now. "He doesn't know that, and a princess won't do."

"You better know what you're doing."

"Oh, I do." He took them to the center of the paddock. He ignored Ben, who had watched them enter the corral with a certain shy caution. Then the horse circled them on feet muffled by snow, and was now tiptoeing along behind them.

Ty turned. Amy, stuck to him like glue, turned with him.

"Ah! I didn't know he was right behind us!" She went to take a step back as the horse pulled up short, but Ty had anticipated it and placed a hand in the middle of her back.

"Don't step back from him," he instructed softly. "Hold your ground. He is reading every single thing about you. He can probably tell your heart is beating too fast. So don't step back. Because if you do, he'll take that as a weakness, that you are less than him, and so he will move forward, claim your space, try to dominate you."

She froze and stared at Ty. He saw the light of understanding go on in the amazing depths of her hazel eyes.

"Oh, my," she whispered, "if that doesn't sound like the story of my life!"

"That's the thing about watching someone with a horse," he told her quietly. "You can tell every single thing about them. How you interact with a horse is exactly how you interact with life."

"Oh, dear."

"Whether you know it or not," Ty finished, "you are telling people how to treat you all the time. Come. Come closer."

He went and stood right at the horse's neck. The baby did not have her hesitancy. He reached eagerly for the horse, buried pudgy fingers in the silken strands of Ben's mane. He cooed his love and approval.

Ty leaned close and blew a gentle breath in the colt's wide nostril. It blew back and he breathed in the scent.

"Try that."

Amy hesitated, studied not the horse, but him, and decided to give him a most fragile gift. She trusted him.

She leaned forward and blew.

And then Ben blew back.

"Breathe it in," Ty said. "Breathe it in. That breath is what you have in common, the thread that connects you both to life. Breathe him in. Can you feel what he is? His essence?"

"His breath is so sweet," she said, awed.

She turned and looked at Ty. Her eyes were shining with that moment of discovery. He knew he had her.

"Okay, now we're going to make the decision it's time for him to leave, so push his shoulder now, and raise your right hand."

The horse moved away from them and out to the perimeter of the corral.

"Keep your eye on his hip, keep your hand up, step toward him."

Fluidly, the horse broke into a relaxed canter and circled them, throwing up great puffs of snow.

"I didn't make him do that!" Amy said, awed.

"Prove to yourself that you did. Back up, lower your right hand and raise your left, and then move one step toward him again."

"I don't have a left!" she reminded him, and wagged her empty sleeve at Ty.

He moved behind her, laughing, and physically lowered her right hand. There was the sweet temptation of her neck again.

"Back up," he instructed.

The horse planted his feet as she backed up, and then Ty picked up the empty sleeve and waved it. Ben swiveled in one graceful move at the switch of hands. He cantered the other way.

"He's so beautiful," Amy said. "I feel as if I'm in a movie."

The horse was beautiful, but his beauty was eclipsed by hers. Her curls were sticking out from under that silly hat, her cheeks were flushed from cold and exhilaration, her eyes were shining. A smile, so genuine it would have outshone the sun, if there had been any sun, played across her lips.

Seeing her with the horse told Ty exactly who she was.

And he knew how right he had been to take the high road with her, to fight the temptation of placing a kiss on the soft curve of her lips or her exposed neck.

Because she was beautiful and soft and gentle to her very core.

In other words, exactly the kind of woman that a

rough-and-tumble guy who had known way too many hard knocks could do a lot of damage to.

Still, enchanted with her reaction to all of this, Ty talked her through the sequence a few more times. Her face was absolutely glowing as she began to understand the horse was responding to her slightest move.

"Everyone and everything is responding to us all the time, at some level. Sometimes it's so subtle we don't know what we've told them."

*For instance, her kiss had told him she was hungry. But her eyes were saying she wasn't ready.*

"Okay, lower your hand—" he let her empty sleeve fall "—and move your eyes to his shoulder."

The horse skidded to a halt. He turned in, his eyes riveted on her. "Step back."

She did, and the horse came into her, dropped his head in front of her in submission that was not surrender.

"Scratch his ears. And his forehead. Say something to him."

"Ben, I think I'm in love with you."

Her voice was husky and sweet, and it seemed to him a man could die to hear such words coming from her.

But his next instructions, intended for the horse, were instructions he needed to heed himself.

"Now turn and walk away."

Not that he could. Not while they were snowed in here together, but there were many ways to walk away.

And he should know because he'd done most of them at one time or another.

"I don't want to walk away," she said, stroking Ben's

nose with soft reverence. "I want to stay like this forever."

Yup, she was the kind of girl who could turn a man's thoughts to forever.

"Sometimes it's better to play hard to get. Turn and walk away," he said more firmly.

She shot him a look, and then did as he asked.

"Don't look back."

"I can feel him," she said. "Ohmygosh, he's breathing right down my neck. Is he following me?"

"Like a dog."

She moved a little faster. She slowed down. She turned, she doubled back on herself. The horse stayed right with her, taking her cues effortlessly, devoted to her as his new leader.

Finally, Ty allowed her to turn and pet Ben some more.

"You were right," she breathed. "Oh, Ty, that was the most fun ever."

"Actually, the most fun is still to come. You think you might like to ride him?"

"Oh," she said, "I don't know."

"I'll ride him, and then you can decide."

He went into the barn and retrieved the tack. He showed her how to brush the horse, was aware of how intent her attention was on him as he saddled and bridled the young colt.

He got on in an easy swing. Now Ty was completely in his world. He felt his own energy and the energy of the colt merging. He felt the balance between them.

He didn't so much ride the horse as dance with him. A few gentle laps around the paddock at a walk, and reversing direction, at a trot. And then, he let the rein loose, gave the slightest pressure with his knees.

The colt moved into an easy lope. He slid him to a halt with pressure and signals that no one could see, that were strictly between him and the horse. They loped the other way.

He glanced at Amy. She was awestruck.

He'd done enough for one day. But what guy didn't love a girl looking at him like that?

He nudged Ben forward, toward the place of freedom. The horse moved out of a lope into a hard gallop. Ty leaned forward, drinking in the air and the scent of the colt. Peripherally he was aware of Amy and the baby in the center.

And it was all one.

A wonderful blur of oneness.

It was a vulnerable moment of choice. He could show her all of who he was, or he could hold back something.

But wasn't the purpose to make her want to be who she truly was?

He dropped the loop of the reins over the saddle horn, and spread his arms wide and tilted his chin up, closing his eyes against the falling snow.

It was complete trust.

Not just in himself. Not just in the horse. Not just in her reaction to all this.

It was complete trust in life.

He lost himself in it, came back only reluctantly. He took up the reins again, and then he stopped and rode the horse into the center, where she was staring at him.

"I have never seen anything like that," she said. "Not ever. I will never forget it as long as I live."

It was like a promise, and he knew he had succeeded in giving her something.

He was aware he had taken a giant risk. He had shown her exactly who he was, and then he knew it had been worth it.

"I want that," she said. "I want to go to that place, be in that place, live in that place."

He bent down and brushed her curls from her face with a gloved fingertip. He realized the baby was probably getting very heavy for her to manage with one arm. He took the baby from her arms and set him in the saddle in front of him. They took a few turns around, and Ty thought of his father again, how some of his earliest memories were of this.

Sitting in the saddle in front of his dad, beginning to understand the language not just of horses, but of his life.

Was it the first time he had consciously realized the gift his father had given him?

What was it about her that was making him see his life in different ways?

He reminded himself of the goal. For her to see her life in a different way. He rode back to her, pulled his leg out of the far stirrup, slid out of the saddle with the baby still in his arms.

"Well, I guess if that's what you want," he said, "you better get on. Because you can't start the trip without finding your ride."

"I don't think I could get on with two good arms," she said doubtfully. "We should wait until I can use both arms. We should wait until it's not snowing. We should—"

"You can always wait. You can always wait until everything is perfect and all the stars line up. But you're going to miss a whole lot of what life is trying to give you right now."

"What if I fall? What if I wreck my other arm. What if—"

He put his finger gently to her lips, and then he set the baby down. He picked her up, two hands around her waist, and lifted.

She was so light that he held her for a moment, like a dancer, or a pairs skater starting a lift.

And then he twisted ever so slightly and put her in the saddle.

"Pick up Jamey," she said. She was clinging to the saddle horn with her visible hand. "He could get stepped on!"

He picked him up, but not before giving her a look that let her know it was his watch, and no babies were getting stepped on on his watch. That horse would not move a muscle without Ty's okay, or some instruction from her.

"I don't want you to be afraid anymore. That's what I want you to take from this. That's what I want you to remember forever. Now pick up the rein with your good hand. Attagirl. Just squeeze him ever so gently with your legs and then release."

The horse walked out. And in front of his eyes, Ty watched as Amy's fear dissolved into something else.

And this time Ty knew he was going to be the one never to forget.

"Whoa, boy," she said a while later as he helped her down, and she watched him strip the saddle and blanket off the horse. "Baking bread is not going to be able to compete with this in the fun department."

"It's going to be whatever we make it," he told her.

And then he looked at the sky. There was no sign of the snow letting up. None. If anything, it seemed to be snowing harder than when they had first come out.

And so there was no sign of their forced togetherness coming to an end.

And that, too, would be whatever they made it.


Ty's house still smelled of fresh-baked bread, even though it had been more than twenty-four hours since they had made it.

The smell alone made his mouth water.

"Do you want some toast," he said, "and jam?"

The baby was bathed and in bed. Ty sprawled out on the couch, his arm thrown up over his forehead, his eyes closed.

Amy turned from the window. "You have not stopped eating since I got here!"

"You have not stopped cooking since you got here."

"We," she reminded him.

"No man who has been cooking for himself as long as I have could resist that bread. Amy, it is the best thing I've ever tasted."

That was not exactly true. The best thing he had ever tasted had been her lips, and after the best part of three days in each other's company, he was fighting himself constantly.

"It's all in the kneading," she said, glanced again at him, something hot flashing through her eyes when he deliberately flexed his kneading muscles for her.

"How do you do this all by yourself?" he asked a few minutes later, coming back into the living room with a plate heaped with toast. "It's utterly exhausting. Who knew a baby was so much work?"

He took a bite, closed his eyes and sighed. Then he reopened them.

"You can't make it stop snowing by standing there."

"I stopped wishing it would stop after you beat me at Scrabble last night. It has to last at least until the rematch. Do you want to set it up for tonight?"

He was happy to see the consistently worried look was gone, even though the continuation of the snowfall meant she wasn't going anywhere tomorrow, either.

He had turned on the radio with supper. What was going on outside his window was a part of what was being called the Storm of the Century. Some of the secondary roads were closed, including The Cowboy Trail, 22, which his driveway joined.

"Honestly, Amy? I'm too tired to pit my wits against you. How do you do it by yourself?"

They were moving back and forth between their two worlds seamlessly. She and the baby had come with him today to do chores. They had all squeezed into the cab of his tractor as he moved large bales into the pasture for his cows. Then they had played with the horse again. Despite not being able to use her one hand, she had executed a pretty passable trot.

Inside, it was her world. She loved to cook. She had shown him how to make bread and cookies, a simple cream soup. The baby was an unbelievable amount of work: diaper and clothing changes, baths and feedings. How did she manage all this by herself?

"It never seems like work to me," she said and came and sat down in the chair opposite him. "It's what I always wanted. Babies. A cozy kitchen. Bread baking."

This was getting easier all the time, too, conversation flowing between them with the ease of old friends.

"What made you want that?" he asked.

She turned and smiled at him. "I know. I know. It's a hopelessly traditional, old-fashioned vision in a modern world. It's not what my parents hoped for me at all."

"Really?" He sensed she was going to trust him with some parts of herself that she did not reveal often.

He needed to be worthy of that trust. He closed his eyes, so he wouldn't look at her lips, and pulled his plate of toast close so that the scent would override hers.

"My parents were both business analysts. Their skills were sought after all over the world. I grew up in Germany, Japan, California, France.

"We always lived in the best houses in the best neighborhoods, but it never felt like home. I don't ever remember having a home-cooked meal, unless our current house came with staff, which they sometimes did. And then it was hardly roast beef and potatoes. Baked Sockeye salmon with a lemongrass sauce.

"I was always in private schools with loads of activities, depending which country we were in. I'm something of a reluctant expert at figure skating, gymnastics, badminton, swimming and soccer. But really, from the youngest age, I remember craving home.

"I craved a sense of family. I was an only child who wanted six brothers and sisters. It was probably unrealistic, my vision based on watching TV families, reading magazines. But unrealistic or not, I started cooking and baking when I was about thirteen. And I had my own ideas about what I wanted my room to look like, wherever we were, and it did not mesh with the designer's idea of *teenage girl*. I wanted homemade crafts on the walls, a crocheted blanket.

"It was my mother's worst nightmare."

Ty laughed. "At thirteen you were crocheting blankets and baking cookies, and that was your mother's worst nightmare? She wouldn't have wanted to know me at thirteen."

"Oh! Tell me about that!"

"Stealing sips of whiskey. Smoking behind the barn. Sneaking out of the house. Taking the truck without permission. Terrorizing the neighborhood girls." He felt the ripple of sympathy for his dad again.

"I'm not saying one more word about my boring childhood!"

"Please?" he wheedled. "I like hearing about you at thirteen."

"I'm not sure why. I taught myself how to cook and crochet. I got a sewing machine and learned to sew. My mother was appalled by my fascination with all things domestic. I had my own little world."

"Boys?" he asked.

"Terrified of them, while writing secret love letters to the ones I liked best. Never mailed, of course."

"Of course." He laughed. He could see her as just that kind of girl: sweet and shy, the kind guys, dumb prisoners to raging hormones that they were, overlooked again and again.

"We were back in Canada when I finished high school—still no boyfriend—and by then, I was dreaming of babies to fill up my little fantasy cottage. But I did what my parents wanted. I went to university in Calgary, as per my mother's plans, but in my second year a boy had finally shown interest in me.

"Poor guy. Before he knew what had happened, I had him cast in the starring role of my secret fantasy. I dropped out to get married. My parents, surprisingly, approved of Edwin, possibly because his family owned a company that traded on the New York Stock Exchange.

"Edwin was still going to university, so we lived with his parents."

"You were newlyweds and you lived with his parents?"

"Actually, at first it seemed as if I was in heaven. His mother was like Martha Stewart on steroids."

"Martha who?"

"Stewart. She has a television show. And a magazine. She's the world's leading expert on all things domestic, from removing wine stains from white linen to making Halloween punch with the illusion of a dismembered hand floating in it."

"Terrifying," he said drily.

"The Halloween punch or Martha?"

"Both. You were telling me about your in-laws."

"They had lived in the same house for twenty-five years."

"That's not long. There have been Hallidays on this place for over a hundred."

Maybe he shouldn't have said that. Amy got a distinctly dreamy look on her face.

"For somebody like me who never had a home, a family in the same place for so long was like a fairy tale coming true. And then it was all about cooking, and stunning crafts, and décor, and creating an environment that whispered sweet welcome.

"But somewhere along the line, I realized it was all about how everything looked, and not about how it felt. Cynthia's perfect home, her perfectly cooked meals, her crystal collections and towels folded in precise thirds—everything looked so perfect and felt so plastic.

"And, I'm afraid that describes my marriage, too. I thought it was the house, so as soon as Edwin finished university, I wanted to move out. But he said it was too much pressure. He'd been appointed CEO of one of the family companies, and that was his life.

"Honestly, I felt as if I was back with my parents. He worked. I was invisible. I thought the baby would help."

"Ah."

"It helped *me*. I didn't feel so alone. I finally had something to live for." She said softly, reluctantly, "It was not what I had hoped my marriage would be."

"My first clue—living with his parents. My second clue—he *wanted* to live with his parents. Pretty hard to chase each other around the house shrieking with *amour* when Mommy and Daddy are looking on."

"We managed to make a baby," she said primly.

"Miracle of miracles."

"I've never said this to another living soul."

He said nothing, waiting.

"The baby was wonderful. Other than that, I've never felt so lonely. My own parents had decided to retire. You know how the type A personality retires? Mountain trekking in Nepal."

"Not there for you."

"You want to hear something ironic? They built an orphanage in Africa."

"And you were practically an orphan."

"I didn't mean to sound like I wanted pity. I had absolutely everything growing up."

"You didn't sound like you wanted pity," he assured her.

"So, almost by accident, after Jamey was born, I started this little website on the internet called Baby Bytes. I never even told Edwin, my parents, his parents. It was so precious to me, and I knew I couldn't handle the put-downs or the patronizing or the criticism or the input.

"Edwin was killed in an accident very shortly after that. He was coming home from work late. He'd had a few drinks and hit a telephone pole.

"I feel like my little company kept me going, gave me back an identity when I was suffocating in everyone's expectations. Their expectations actually felt even more stifling after he died.

"I was supposed to behave like the grieving widow for the rest of my life. Live with his parents. Gratefully accept their help and their gifts.

"When the house-sitting opportunity came up, I knew I had to take it. To make the break. Baby Bytes has started to make money, and I know I can take it to the next level."

"Tell me about it."

She gave him a wary look, as if she was deciding whether or not to tell him the color of her underwear.

"It's just a website. It's free for people to use, mostly young moms. It's got recipes on it for everything from making bread to making your own baby food. And I put up patterns for clothes and homemade toys. Photography tips. I have little contests for cute baby pictures and best names. Nobody is more surprised than me by the number of people using the site."

She ducked her head, as if waiting for him to mock her success.

"I think that's great," he said, and he meant it.

"It's kind of like the Martha Stewart of the baby world," she said, her tone self-disparaging.

He hated that. When no one else put her down, she did it herself.

"I like how you are blending different worlds," he told her. "Using high tech to showcase things you value."

He was aware that was what they had been doing for the past few days, too. Blending worlds. Moving back and forth between each other's worlds with a growing amount of comfort.

"I started putting out feelers," she confided shyly, "and a couple of the big baby companies, like Baby Nap, have committed to taking out ads on it. It's going to give me a very comfortable living within a year."

"So you have your parents' business acumen, too. That's amazing. You must be very proud."

"I'm scared."

"No, you're not. You were scared, but today and yesterday you played with a horse. And now you don't have to be scared anymore. Not of anything."

"Anything?" she whispered. She took a deep breath, and turned, and looked at him with those amazing, beautiful eyes. "How about the fact it's still snowing?"

"I think we'll survive."

"It's the twenty-first of December today. How about the fact I may be spending Christmas with you?"

"It's just another day. You can celebrate it however you want when you leave."

She looked at him long and hard, as if he was clearly missing the point. She drew in another deep breath.

He had to have known this was coming. He had to have sensed it in their growing comfort with one another, the effortless way he had become her extra hand, the enthusiastic way she was embracing his world.

But somehow her next words shocked him completely. Completely.

"How about the way I'm starting to feel about you, Ty Halliday? How about that?"

# CHAPTER SIX

TY leaped up off the couch as if he'd accidentally sat on a hot ember. He nearly dumped his plate.

"Like I said, I'm exhausted. Done in. I have to go to bed."

Amy squinted at him narrowly. This was a repeat of when she had kissed him! He was letting her know, in no uncertain terms, he was not interested in her in *that* way.

"I'm going to have to figure out a way to get to my dad tomorrow," he said as if he had to rush off to bed and think hard about that.

"Your dad?" she asked, astounded.

"He and his lady friend live on the old Halliday homestead place. It's a few miles from here. I'd better make sure they're stocked up."

Amy felt shocked. She'd assumed Ty was alone in life. Really alone. As alone as any person she had ever met. But his dad lived a few miles away, and he'd never even mentioned it?

She suddenly felt embarrassed that she had blurted out her whole life story to him. In fact, over the past three days, she had revealed quite a bit about herself.

But he hadn't! She had just assumed they were getting to know each other, but in actual fact he'd been getting to know her.

Enough to know he wasn't interested in *that* way. She watched him take off down the hall to his room, heard the finality in the way the door snapped closed.

Ty Halliday was telling her to back off and that was his right.

It was the situation here that had made her feel so instantly enamored with him. It was seeing him laughing with Jamey, frowning over the Scrabble board, kneading bread until his arm muscles rippled, looking after her hand with such tenderness, stepping up to the plate to uncomplainingly shoulder every single thing she couldn't do because of her injury.

But the kicker had been to see Ty Halliday on a horse. It went beyond horsemanship.

It went straight to spirit.

She had witnessed the grace and the power of man and horse melt into one seamless entity.

Watching Ty ride was going to that place she had been to so rarely: a place of being fully engaged, fully connected, fully alive.

And she thought she might as well just die now if she did not learn how to get there, too.

But it was precisely the same mistake she had made before. She was looking for a hero, someone to rescue her from her life.

And Ty would certainly fit anyone's definition of a hero. Seeing him in his element and watching the ease with which he had slipped into hers, given the forced closeness of their circumstances, her total reliance on him, it was natural that she would be feeling things with a strange and sizzling intensity.

It was not unlike a hostage bonding with their captor.

And if there was one thing she was done with, it was being taken hostage. She had to take responsibility for her own life. No more waiting to be rescued.

Knowing exactly what she had to do, she marched into the kitchen.

The phone was still unplugged from the wall.

So, despite the physical closeness of his father, Ty really was more alone than most people. She doubted he had even given a thought to his phone being un-plugged—him being unable to be reached—since he had pulled that thing from the wall. If he was concerned about his father, why didn't he phone him?

None of her business, she told herself firmly. She was in no position to advise Ty on family matters when she had allowed her own to become such a mess.

Now, taking a deep breath, Amy plugged the tele-phone back in and dialed the familiar number. She was aware her heart was beating too fast. She was aware that all her life she had been telling people how to treat her.

Now she had ridden a horse. Now she had breathed his essence deep inside her. Now she had to step up and claim her own space.

"Hello, Cynthia, it's Amy."

"I have been so worried! I was within a hairbreadth of calling the police."

Cynthia's tone was wounded, and of course she would not have called the police. It was just her way of letting Amy know she felt her negligence was nearly criminal. She bit back the impulse to apologize.

Instead, she pictured walking up to that horse and not giving an inch.

"Cynthia," she said firmly, "while I appreciate your concern, I'm fine. Jamey is fine. I just wanted to let you know we won't be there for Christmas dinner. You've probably seen on the news that the roads are closed out this way. I'm at the end of a long driveway. It's going to take a while to dig out."

"But where are you? The call display still says Halliday, not McFinley. You said you were house-sitting for people called McFinley. I've called the number listed for them in the phone book. And there is no answer. And there is no answer at the house you called from with the so-called washer repairman. So where are you? And who was that man who answered the phone? Please don't play me for the fool. I know it wasn't a washer repairman. Have you met someone on the internet? It's not safe!"

A thousand explanations ran through Amy's head, and then feeling sweet relief she realized she did not have to make any of them.

"Cynthia, I need you to listen carefully. I love you and I appreciate your concern for me and for Jamey. But I am an adult woman. I do not need to report to you."

"Please just come back!"

"I won't be coming back. Not to live there."

"But John and I are in such a comfortable position to look after you."

"I don't want to be looked after."

"Think of Jamey! We are in a far better position to give him everything he could ever want than you will ever be!"

There it was, what was always there: the underlying lack of faith in her.

"Cynthia, I want to be respected. I want to look after myself."

There was a long pause. "Really, Amy, this is no time to make a philosophical stand. The well-being of my grandson is at stake."

Truer words had never been spoken. And Amy did not want to teach her son that she could not stand on her own two feet, that she was a dependent personality without the guts or the wherewithal to make it on her own.

Ty Halliday had just done her a big favor by rejecting her interest in him! He'd set her back on the correct path.

"Jamey will miss you on Christmas. We'll come for a visit as soon as the weather permits." As she hung up on her mother-in-law, Amy felt she had never been more on her own path.

She heard Ty get up in the morning, rustling around. She had the feeling he was trying very hard not to wake her.

And the woman she had been when she first arrived probably would have rolled over and pretended to sleep until he left the house, leaving her to nurse her wounded ego.

But she was not that woman anymore. She got out of bed, looked out her window for a moment, then donned her dressing gown and went into the kitchen.

Ty was actually glaring at the coffeepot, drumming the countertop with impatient fingers waiting for it to brew. The radio was on at a very low volume next to him.

He looked up at her, looked away, clearly not happy

to see her. He removed the pot and stuck his travel mug directly under the drip.

She ordered herself to face it head-on. "Look, Ty, I just looked out my window. Still snowing. We're going to be stuck here together for a few more days."

He nodded, put the cup to his lips. "Yeah, I saw the snow, too. The road reports are the only thing on the radio. Some roads are open, but there are travel advisories on them and the weather warnings haven't been lifted."

"So, you're stuck with me."

He winced and rolled his shoulders uncomfortably, but didn't argue with her blunt wording.

"Ty, I don't want you to feel uncomfortable in your own home. I'm not going to break into pieces because you made it clear you don't find me attractive. You've done me a favor, actually. I should be all done looking for heroes."

He choked on the coffee. He set down the cup. He stalked over to her.

"Don't find you attractive? Are you crazy?"

She looked up at him, drank in the fire in those sapphire eyes, the way his pulse beat in his throat, the tight line of his jaw.

"I find you way too attractive, Amy."

"You do?" For a moment, she felt her whole world start to shift, but then she reminded herself that the new Amy Mitchell needed to be more cynical, more pragmatic. "Or you're just saying that?"

His mouth fell open. His eyes spit blue sparks of pure heat. "I don't just say things. How can you not know that about me?"

"We hardly know each other at all. It feels as if we do because of how we've been forced together, but I shouldn't have said what I said last night. It put you in an awkward position. But don't worry, I don't plan to moon over you."

He moved in closer, his eyes still burning with a deep blue flame, like the one that hovered over the hottest part of a fire. And then his hand moved, almost as if it were against his will, and his finger traced the line of her mouth before his hand went to the back of her head and buried itself in her curls. He drew her close.

The blue fire that had been in his eyes sizzled briefly in the small space between them, singeing the air, making her lips tingle.

"Oh, Amy," he whispered, and then he took her lips with his.

Inferno.

It was everything she had known it would be, and it was so much more.

As his lips, remarkably soft, astoundingly sensual, claimed hers, her world made the final melt into his.

The touch of his lips intensified, took charge and then surrendered to her. He was gentle, and fierce and hungry. He was tender and ruthless, taking and giving.

It seemed to her his kiss asked her not to submit to him, but to be worthy of him. And so she gave back. Everything. For the first time in her life, she gave every single thing she was. Her gentleness. Her fury. Her hunger. Her uncertainty. Her yearning. Her dreams. Her strength.

When it seemed as if there would be nothing left of

either of them except smoldering ash, Ty pulled back from her.

He took a step back. His shoulders were heaving as he raked his hand through his hair, tossed her a troubled look.

She took a step toward him, not ready to let go.

He took a step back from her.

"Amy, we are in a complicated situation here. It is incredibly intense. Giving in to this will only make it way more complicated. That's what I was trying to tell you last night when I walked away. Now, I'm going to my dad's. I'll be gone a couple of hours and that should give me a chance to cool off and put my head back on straight."

Terrible to be so thrilled that she was responsible for the fact he did not have his head on straight.

"How are you getting to your dad's in all this snow? Why don't you just phone him?"

"It's complicated."

"Hmm. For a simple cowboy you seem to have a complicated life."

"Some days are worse than others." His eyes trailed to her lips, and then moved swiftly away. He jammed his coffee mug back under the drip, waited for it to fill partially, then took a huge swig. He was going to burn his mouth on that coffee if he didn't watch out.

"I've got a sleigh. I'll hook up a couple of the big horses to it, put a few supplies in, in case he needs them."

"I'm coming."

"I just said we need to cool off."

"I'll try to keep my hands off you. But, Ty, I am not missing a genuine sleigh ride for anything."

Ty looked torn, but then he gave in. It was not like him to give in so easily, and she felt her heart warm as much as it had for the kiss. He *wanted* to share this experience with her and Jamey. Their worlds were not yet finished melting together.

"Now, what do you think your dad might need? We'll bring him the last loaf of fresh bread and—"

"He doesn't need the last loaf of fresh bread," Ty said sourly.

"Ty! We can always make more."

But he still looked sour as she found a box and with her good hand started loading a few basic supplies, including the fresh bread, into it. Jamey woke, and without being asked, Ty disappeared down the hall.

When he came out the baby had already been changed and was in a fresh Onesies.

An hour later, with Ty carrying Jamey in his little blue snowsuit, they made their way down to the barn. The snow was still coming. But did it seem a little lighter this morning?

Handing Jamey to her at the barn, Ty left them. He returned with two horses, one lead rope in each hand, and brought them through the open barn doors. The horses were absolutely huge, golden-colored with heavy white manes and tails, and white feathers around their feet.

"Their feet must be as big as pie plates!" she said.

Maybe her awareness had been heightened by that kiss, but every single thing seemed to shimmer this morning.

She was so aware: Ty in a sheepskin-lined jean jacket, dark cowboy hat, leather gloves, looking strong and rugged and calm and self-assured—the quintessential cowboy. And the horses: clouds of breath, the warm smell of them, the squeak and jingle of the leather harnesses as Ty got them ready.

"Can I breathe in their noses?" she said. "The way I did with Ben?"

He cast her a glance from under the shadowed brim of his cowboy hat. After that kiss she was aware of him trying frantically to rebuild walls. But she did not miss the quiet satisfaction that passed through his eyes that she was not afraid of these huge horses.

She went and stood at their shoulders, breathed in their wonderful scent, let Jamey pet and stroke and coo and call out in excitement.

But all the time, she was so aware of how Ty was with the horses. She had promised not to moon over him, but really, how could she stop herself?

Besides, he was very focused on what he was doing, ignoring her. This was second nature to him. Ty worked around the huge animals with confidence and unconscious grace, entirely certain of himself. He talked to them as he quickly brushed them out, his tone low and soothing, his voice sending shivers up and down her spine.

The harnesses seemed complicated, and yet Ty's manner was easy. Putting a harness on a horse was no different for him than checking the air pressure on a tire or the dipstick on the oil was for most men.

And yet watching a man doing mundane vehicle maintenance could never have this kind of pull to it.

Watching Ty get the horses ready, his hands gliding along strong muscles, working buckles, untangling leather straps, was like watching something extraordinarily and breathtakingly beautiful. It was a symphony of motion and energy.

When he had the horses harnessed, he led them out into the snow. Bells jingled on the big leather collars and the snow kicked out in huge puffs from their feathered feet.

There was a lean-to attached to the barn, and in it was a huge lump under a blue tarp. He dropped the reins for the horses.

"Stand," he commanded, and the huge horses stood quietly, while he went and removed the tarp.

Again, she felt as if she was in a state of heightened awareness, because the sleigh was so pretty it made her eyes smart with tears.

It was possibly the most Christmassy thing she had ever seen. It was painted bright red, with a black leather front seat and shiny runners.

Expertly, Ty backed the horses toward the hitch. Again, watching his confidence and efficiency of motion took her breath away. Once the horses were hitched, he took the baby, helped her up onto the seat and climbed up beside her.

He took up the reins. "Hang on." He made a clicking noise. The sleigh lurched as it moved from the dry ground under the roof to the snow outside the lean-to. And then it was gliding along, the huge horses plowing effortlessly through the deep snow, tossing their heads, moving into a huge-gaited trot.

Ty directed them up the hill to the house, dropped

the reins and told the horses to stand. He made several trips: the box of supplies, baby things, warm blankets which he stowed behind the seat. And then lastly he came out with several square items wrapped in towels.

"I threw a couple of bricks in the oven this morning after you said you were coming. Just tuck them around you and Jamey."

She did and the sensation of warmth on this chilly day was incredible. The sensation of being cared about was even more incredible.

Though, she reminded herself, he would have denied it. If she questioned it, she was sure he would say it was something he would do for anyone.

Ty got back in the driver's seat, took up the reins and moved the sleigh down the slope of his hill, where his driveway once had been. At the bottom of the hill, he turned along a wooden fence line.

"This is called a pioneer fence," he said. "My great-grandfather built it."

The snow falling was even lighter now, and the horses settled into the task at hand, bells jingling, their great strength breaking a path through the snow effortlessly. The runners on the sleigh made a hissing noise on the ground. The baby laughed and all those sounds became part of the magic of a world muffled by snow.

"I think," Amy whispered, "this may be the most beautiful moment of my whole life."

Ty shot her a look that clearly said *sheltered,* but it didn't matter. The horse-drawn sleigh followed the fence for a while, and then Ty turned and they wove their way through open fields, then through a small forested stretch. When they came out the sun had burst through and was glinting off the pristine snow.

But it wasn't white. It was like the earth was covered in sparkling diamonds with blue fire at their core.

"Don't get your hopes up about the snow stopping," Ty said.

But somewhere along the way, Amy realized, all that had shifted. She didn't want it to stop. She wanted it to snow forever, to stay in this world of the two of them, and the baby, and Scrabble and baking bread together, and squeezing into the cab of his tractor and playing with horses.

"Why do you say that?"

"I can taste more snow on the air."

She stared at him. "You can taste snow on the air?"

"Sure, try it."

And so she stuck out her tongue, and tasted nothing. And then she breathed the air in through her mouth. Still nothing.

And then she noticed his shoulders shaking with suppressed mirth.

"You can't taste it!" she said, thumping him firmly on the arm.

He rubbed his arm with pretend hurt. "Yes, I can. But I also heard it on the radio. Slight clearing today, more snow coming."

And somehow the tension that had been created by that kiss dissipated, and there was something playful and comfortable in the air between them.

"You want to try driving the horses?" he asked.

"Really? How can I with one hand?"

"We'll figure it out."

Amy was so aware that woman she had been when she'd arrived would have shrunk back from this. Would have seen everything that could go wrong: horses stampeding, sleigh overturning.

Now she felt eager for the new experience, warmed that Ty offered it to her, trusted her not to screw up.

Ty took the baby and passed her the reins into her one hand. She could feel the power of the horses singing through the leather. She laughed out loud. She was aware of Ty watching her, a small smile tickling across the line of his lips.

A woman could start living to make that man smile, to make that light go on in his eyes!

"Just keep your hand steady, just like that. We're going that way." He reached over and pulled ever so slightly on the inside rein, his hand brushing hers, and then staying there.

Amy suspected the horses knew exactly where they were going, but it was so much fun anyway, like taking a trip into the past. This is what life had once been, there had been a beautiful simplicity to it, moments that were slower and lovelier. She felt as if her whole body was humming with awareness.

Though, of course, Ty was a big part of that. His shoulder brushing hers, his gloved hand resting on her mitten, the baby happy in his lap, his face relaxed and happy, his laughter frequent.

She couldn't taste snow coming, but somehow the taste of him, the way his lips had been on hers, was still with her, woven into the magic of the day.

Woven into who she was becoming, and who she would always be, now.

They moved up a hill, crested it, traveled along the ridge for a bit, and then he took the reins back from her as they headed down through a small copse of trees.

When they came out of the trees, they were partway down a valley, in rolling open pasture. Spread below them was a scene from a Christmas card: an old barn, wood grayed from weather, sagging from age and hard use.

And there was a house.

It was a two-story log house, the logs weathered as gray as the barn. A low porch wrapped around the entire place. Smoke curled out of a river rock chimney.

Amy could see bright curtains in the windows and cheerful light inside. Even from here she could see an immense wreath on the front door, and the porch railings decorated with festive red bows.

"Stop, Ty, please stop."

He sent her a puzzled look, but did as she asked. She passed him the baby and climbed from the sled, stood in the snow, gazing down at the house below her.

The horses turned their heads to look at her, curious about the stop.

"Stand."

Ty came with Jamey and stood beside her.

"What is it?" he asked quietly.

She took in a deep breath, looked at him, this self-assured man holding her baby as if it was second nature to him.

She debated telling him. It made her feel as if she was showing him something that would make her so vulnerable.

But, she reminded herself, the new Amy was courageous.

And that didn't just mean taking the reins.

It meant risking showing people your heart. It meant doing that, even though she was risking rejection—again. She felt compelled to tell him who she really was.

"Oh, Ty," she breathed, "all my life I dreamed of home. All my life. And that is what I dreamed of." She gestured to the scene below them.

He could have done anything. He could have been impatient. Or mocked her. But instead, she felt his hand on her shoulder, the gentle squeeze of fingers under his gloves.

He gave her his silence and let her drink her fill of the beautiful scene. And then he helped her back on the sleigh and they made the final descent to the house.

As they got closer, it got better. Ty pulled the big horses to a halt at the wide steps that went up to the front door. There was actually a hitching post there, and he got down from the sleigh, fastened the horses, and then came back and took Jamey before helping her down.

The wreath on the door was thick, lush with different types of boughs all woven together. It had a huge plaid bow on it, and country ornaments—rocking horses and snowmen with cowboy hats—peeked out from under the boughs. There was a little wooden word buried in the bows.

*Wish.*

As they went up the steps, she could smell the fragrance of the wreath. It reminded her of how close it was to Christmas. Despite the tree at Ty's house, she had not been able to achieve any kind of Christmassy feeling there.

The door opened before they knocked, and Amy's sense of somehow coming home was complete. A woman stood there, diminutive, white-haired, her face etched, not with surprise, but with kindness.

Behind her wood floors glowed with the patina of age, and a fireplace, hung with socks, crackled with bright welcome. *Wish*. This was exactly what Amy had always wished for.

"Ty!" the woman said, "what a nice surprise."

"Beth."

Amy turned to him, taken aback by something cold in his tone and in his eyes. This is what she should have known all along: Ty was not interested in being part of Amy's picture of perfection.

"Oh, my word," Beth said reverently, holding out her arms. If she had noticed Ty's coldness, she did not acknowledge it. "You've brought us a baby."

Ty handed off the baby into the eager arms, turned around and clattered back down the steps.

"Hunter, look! Ty's come and he's brought company. Come in. Come in."

Amy stepped in the door. And saw Ty's father. She would have known it was him instantly, not so much because they looked alike but because of the way he held himself. He was extraordinarily handsome even though his hair was white as snow and his features were weathered. He was in a wheelchair, but even so, he exuded power, his energy was like a brilliant light in the room.

His features were stern, and there was wariness in his dark eyes, but when he saw the baby it melted. Beth brought Jamey to him, and he held out his arms and took him. Amy had never seen a man so at ease with a baby. Certainly Edwin had never acquired this ease, and her father-in-law was like a stick man when he found Jamey in his arms.

But Ty's father was obviously a man who knew a great deal about babies.

*My mother left when I was about that age.*

Ty came back in the door and set the box of supplies inside of it. "I thought you might be needing a few things."

Their eyes locked, the young man and the old.

Hunter spoke, his tone proud. "We were just fine."

The tension was raw in the room, and Amy suddenly understood why Ty had not phoned and had acquiesced so easily to her coming.

His offer to help would have been refused. And he had brought her because she would provide the distraction.

"I'm Amy Mitchell," she said, kicking off her boots. Her hand was taken by Beth.

"Amy, I'm Beth, and this is Hunter."

She went over to Ty's dad. She loved how he was with the baby. He was already engrossed in removing the snowsuit, and Jamey was enthralled with him.

"Papa, papa, papa," he crowed as if he had met a long-lost love.

She extended her hand, and it was swallowed in one that was rough textured and as strong as his son's. His eyes searched her face, and then he let go of her hand, a small smile playing the stern line of his mouth.

"I'm Hunter Halliday."

"Tea or coffee?" Beth called.

Ty was still standing at the door, holding the first box of supplies. He looked as if he planned to just drop it off and leave!

"Tea," Amy said. She wasn't leaving this place for as long as she could help it. The sensation of coming home had intensified, not diminished, since she had come in that door.

Ty made a growling noise deep in his throat. "I'll see to the horses." And then he turned and went back out the door.

Amy loved it at the old homestead. She loved the handmade throw rugs on the wide-planked floors, the scarred centuries-old harvest table, the crackling fire in the fireplace. She loved the worn furniture and the paned windows. She loved the cat curled up on the hearth. She loved the smell in the air, the tart scent of the pine boughs, a hint of wood smoke, the delicious aroma of something baking.

She shrugged off her coat, and Beth made a fuss about her bandaged hand and clucked sympathetically when Amy told her what had happened.

"I was a nurse before I retired. Do you mind if I look at it?"

Baby in his lap, Hunter wheeled over to the table. So, while he found a set of keys and entertained the baby with them, Amy sat down and Beth looked at her hand.

"Ty did a great job on this. It looks fine. I'll just change the dressing."

Amy was aware she was in the company of strangers, and yet she felt safe and loved and entirely at home.

Ty stood in the doorway, surveying the scene, his face impassive. "What do you need done?" he said to Beth.

His father answered. "I can do it myself."

Ty blew out an impatient breath, went back out the door. A few seconds later they heard an ax thumping into wood. It managed to sound quite angry.

"So," Beth said, setting a teapot on the table—most likely antique—and scones steaming from the oven, "what brings you to Halliday Creek Ranch, Amy?"

And while Hunter broke scones into bits and fed them to Jamey, who opened his mouth and cooed like a small eager bird, she found herself telling them. And not feeling the least ashamed of her ineptitude with the GPS device.

Beth and Hunter seemed to think her descending by accident on Ty was one of the most hilarious stories they had ever heard.

When Ty came back through the door, his arms loaded with freshly split wood, he found them all laughing. Looking like thunder, he dumped the wood in the wood box by the fireplace and went back out the door.

They heard the angry bite of the ax blade into wood again.

The next hour was a delight of laughter and easy conversation. But in the background Amy was aware of Ty's seething presence. Ty chopped wood and filled the wood box to overflowing. Then he climbed up on the porch roof and cleared snow. When he was done that, they could see him out the window, heaving snow off the path to the garage.

When he finally came back in, he had worked himself into such a sweat that steam rose off him.

"Amy, we should go."

"I was hoping you'd stay for lunch," Beth said.

"Maybe another time," Ty said. Polite. Terse.

His father glanced at him.

And Amy saw clearly a whole gamut of emotions going through the elder Halliday's eyes. Pride. And something deeper than pain. Sorrow.

How could Ty be like this? So stubborn? So indifferent to the pain he was causing people?

What had happened between this father and son? And was there any chance, any chance at all, that maybe she could help fix it? So that they all could experience a Christmas miracle?

# CHAPTER SEVEN

"WHAT happened to your dad?" Amy asked.

The horses were more eager to get home than they had been to leave, and it was necessary to have a firm hand on the reins to keep them in check. The snow was falling lightly again, too.

Ty glanced at her. He was aware that she hadn't wanted to leave his dad and Beth, aware of the reproving look she had cast at him when he'd refused lunch.

His father had worked his charm on her. The old bastard could be charming when he set his mind to it. He'd never been short of female companionship.

"He's an old-style cowboy," Ty said, stripping his voice of any emotion. "They bronced out horses. Throw a saddle on a green colt, let him buck it out, put it to work right away, work the knots out as you go. It's dumb. And dangerous. But you could never tell my dad anything. He knew it all. And then one day he met a horse who had more buck than he had stick."

"It must be very hard on a man who lived like that to make the adjustment to being in a wheelchair," Amy said.

Her voice begged him to show some sympathy.

Instead, he just shrugged.

"What's wrong between you two, Ty?"

Her voice was so soft, her eyes so warm. Inviting him to lay it at her feet. Inviting him to share his burdens.

He had seen that word *wish* peeking out from the dark green of Beth's wreath.

And he was aware, in a very short time, that's what Amy had done to his world. Breathed life into a wish he thought he had managed to kill a long time ago.

With her Christmas tree and her filling his house with the smells of baking, with her enthusiasm to try new things, with her soft voice, and her wit and her intelligence, and her unguarded tenderness toward the baby, she was making him wish for a different life.

But he'd done that when he was a kid. Wished and wished and wished.

Around Christmas, he had wished even harder. There was magic in the air. And joy. Unexpected gifts. In these country communities, Christmas was a big deal. Community events, baking marathons, sleigh rides, home decorating contests, neighbors gathering, tables groaning under the weight of food.

He and his father had always been included in everything. They had so many invitations for Christmas dinner they were always left with a hard choice of where to go.

But instead of soothing him, being included in other people's family Christmases had only made Ty more aware of his own lack, so aware of the warmth and good cheer that other people's families brought them.

And so he had wished harder.

But his wishes had never come true. And then, the night his father had given him that pack of letters, when he was seventeen, that place in him that had fostered hope had died.

Or at least he thought it had.

Now he could clearly see that an ember of that hope had remained. He could clearly see that Amy could fan it back to life.

But he had no desire to have it live again, to be open to the world of pain and disappointment that empty wishes brought.

"Amy," he said, his voice deliberately cold, "don't go there."

She flinched as if he had slapped her, and he wanted to take it back. He wanted to tell her everything.

But it felt like a weakness.

And there was no room for weakness in a world without hope. None at all. And yet he found the recrimination in her eyes hard to bear. Maybe if he showed her those letters and told her all of it, maybe then she would get it.

He hazarded a glance at her. Jamey was fast asleep, snuggled into her breast.

Amy was a picture of softness.

She was looking at the world, snow falling again, the steam coming from the horses' nostrils in giant puffs, with a certain rapt attention, as if it was all miraculous.

"There's absolutely no chance I'm going to get away before Christmas, is there?" she asked, worried.

Maybe she was getting it after all, figuring out she was going to be spending Christmas with him, and that he was hard-hearted and a Christmas grinch, and it wasn't going to be much fun at all.

"It doesn't look like it," he said.

"Then I have a lot to do to get ready," she said. "Tomorrow is Christmas Eve!"

He saw he had misread her worry. It wasn't about having Christmas with him. It was about making Christmas what she wanted it to be. She was determined to have Christmas wherever she was.

"Don't get too uptight about it," he said. "It's just another day."

"No, Ty," she said firmly. "It isn't."

He dropped her off at the house, carrying the baby in for her. And then he took the horses down to the barn. It didn't take him long to get them unharnessed, and to do his evening chores.

It didn't take him long at all, and yet when he came back the transformation of his house had already started.

"Ty, before you take your coat off, could you go cut me some boughs? I'd love to bring the scent in here. I can make a simple centerpiece for the table with tree boughs and a candle."

*Tell her no,* Ty ordered himself. But he found he couldn't. It wasn't as if it was her choice to be here. She was stuck here. She wanted to make the best of it. For her baby.

Heaving a big sigh, Ty went back outside and began cutting boughs.

"I didn't need that many," she said when he came back in.

Nonetheless, she looked delighted as she spread out the boughs on the kitchen counter and began to sort through them.

"Do you smell them, Ty?" she asked, smiling over her shoulder.

"Yeah."

"Take off your coat. Come help me. Darn this burned hand. I can't do anything."

Again, he knew he should say no. For his own self-preservation, it seemed imperative.

But he didn't want to be the one to put out the light in her face. And it was true. She was going to need his help.

If she had enough time with him, he would eventually manage to snuff out her light, he was sure. But for right now, why not just be the better man? Reach deep inside and make it not about him, but about her and Jamey?

"Okay," he said gruffly. "Show me what to do."

And as she showed him, something in him relaxed. He allowed her enthusiasm to touch him. And then, he gave himself over to it.

They decorated the house with boughs until the scent filled every corner. Then they ate, bathed the baby, read bedtime stories together, the baby between them on the narrow bed in the guest room grabbing at pages.

When Jamey was finally in bed, she started ticking things off on her fingers. "So, Christmas Eve. I want to make a gingerbread house. I want that to be one of Jamey's and my traditions. His grandmother, Cynthia, makes the most gorgeous gingerbread creations. Last year, we did a little village together. Maybe I should start the gingerbread tonight." She glanced at the clock, worried that she was running out of time.

"I am pretty sure there is nothing in my kitchen to make a gingerbread house, never mind a gingerbread village."

"Oh, I brought everything I need."

"Where the heck did you hide the trailer you must have hauled behind that car to get all your stuff here?"

"I'm very organized. I have a talent for spatial relationships. I bet I could figure out how to get an elephant inside that car if I had to."

"Let's hope you never have to," he said deadpan.

"We could be done in an hour. The cookie part. And then it will be cool enough to cut it and make the house tomorrow."

"I don't want to make gingerbread." A man had to put his foot down, or he'd be swept up in her world before he quite knew what had hit him. The truth was, he didn't want to make gingerbread tonight. Or tomorrow, either. A gingerbread village? No thanks to that much Christmas hokiness.

"I could probably do it myself," she said, but doubtfully, glaring down at her wrapped hand with accusation. "I will do it myself."

"Oh, never mind. I'll give you a hand." It was a surrender.

"You will?"

"One house. No village." But not a complete surrender.

They were not done in an hour. His cranky oven burned the first batch of gingerbread black. Finally, the gingerbread, perfect and golden-brown, was cooling on his kitchen counter.

"There," Amy said, satisfied. "I'm out of your hair. Do whatever you would normally do. Pretend I'm not here."

Good idea. He went into the living room, settled in his chair and picked up his book.

His house smelled overpoweringly of pine boughs and gingerbread. There was a Christmas tree in his living room. And baby toys all over the floor.

And then there was Amy, sitting across from him, looking out the window. "Still snowing."

"Uh-huh." He scrunched lower in his chair, furrowed his brow. But try as he might, he could not pretend she wasn't there. And who knew when he might have an opportunity like this again?

"What the heck is a dactylic hexameter?"

She looked thoughtful. "I have no idea."

And then they were both laughing.

"I always read two books at once," he told her. "One that's really hard, and one for pure enjoyment."

She came and sat beside him, and he read a few passages of the epic poem to her.

She wrinkled her nose. "Could we try the pure enjoyment one?"

"I'm so happy you asked," he said, and then he went and got *Lonesome Dove* and read her his favorite part of that. And somehow they were talking and talking and talking, and they fell asleep on the couch with her head nestled against his chest.

He woke up to her stirring against him.

She opened her eyes, looked at him groggily, and then smiled the most beautiful smile he had ever seen.

"It's Christmas Eve," she said, as round-eyed and full of wonder as a child.

"Technically, that would be tonight."

She thumped him on his chest with her small fist, a good-natured reprimand.

"We have so much to do! We have to make the gingerbread house. Jamey will love helping with that." Suddenly, she went very still. "Do you have a turkey? That should come out of the freezer today."

"I don't have a turkey. Sorry."

"A chicken, then?"

"Sorry, my freezer is full of what I raise, which is beef."

"Somehow I can't imagine a big steak for Christmas dinner," she said.

"I can."

He got the thump again. Funny, the things that could make a man realize he was losing control.

He went out and did the chores. When he came back in, Jamey was awake and needing tending, and Amy was champing at the bit to get her gingerbread house made.

Then with her instructions, he was taking the sheets of gingerbread and cutting them.

"Now, we make a house."

He did not want to think of making a house with Amy. It felt as if thoughts could make him weak instead of strong.

"We use this icing to glue it all together."

Carefully, Ty cut the sheets of cookie into squares. Even being careful, a nice chunk broke off. It was a reminder that he could not be trusted to make any kind of a house with anyone.

He popped the broken piece into his mouth, passed some to the grasping baby.

"Hey, it's not to eat," she said, and he popped a piece into her open mouth to silence her.

Focused intently, he took the slabs of cookie and stood four of them up, leaning on each other to form rough walls. Then, pleased, he put another on top.

"Well?" He stood back and surveyed his house.

"It doesn't look like a house, Ty."

"What does it look like?"

"I don't know. A box."

"I'll fix the roof." He took another piece of gingerbread, took a bite out of it, and then made a slanted roof instead of a flat one.

"I told you, it's not to eat! Did you have to take a bite out of the roof? It looks like—"

"Hansel and Gretel have been here," he decided happily. It looked like the whole thing was leaning, ready to topple over. He slathered the joints liberally with the icing glue. It got all over the place, including his hands. He handed the wooden spoon to Jamey, who merrily chewed the end and then bashed the kitchen counter with it.

She eyed the house critically after he'd made the changes. "Now it looks like a shed."

"Perfect. Just what I planned. A manger for Christmas."

The thump again.

"Hey, I'm a cowboy, not a construction guy."

And not anyone who could be trusted to make a house with her.

He made a few adjustments. "It will look fine once we add a few windows."

But of course it didn't look fine. Jamey had to "help"

decorate, and the jelly beans and jujubes that didn't make it into his mouth were rather mutilated by the time they made it onto the house.

She stepped back from it.

She surveyed the house: listing badly, part of the roof broken, misshapen candies on it, and then she looked at her baby, sticky with icing and gingerbread, and then she looked at Ty.

And it was as if that scent that filled his house and made it home was right inside of him when she looked at him like that.

She started to laugh. "It's perfect," she declared.

Amy stared at the house, and let the feeling it was giving her fill her up. Perfection.

It was not the kind of house Cynthia made—perfect miniatures from a Swiss village. In fact, it looked only remotely like a house.

It had a bite out of the roof. The candies were sliding in icing down the walls into a heap at the bottom. The whole thing was tilting quite badly to one side, and looked as if it might fall right over.

And for all that it looked wrong?

It had never felt so right. Christmas had never felt so right as it did in this moment, sharing a room with that big golden-haired cowboy, watching his eyes tilt with laughter as he used his finger to clean icing off Jamey's nose.

Her other Christmas Eve activities were perfect, too. Ty dug an old sled out of the barn, so they went down the hill in front of his house, sinking in the deep snow, inching along, tumbling and laughing. The snow also was not quite right for making a snowman, not nearly sticky enough, and they ended up with a lumpy pile with an old cowboy hat sitting on top of it, two rocks for eyes and a carrot for a nose.

What the snow was perfect for was snow angels, and they soon covered that entire slope with the imprints of their bodies.

Her feeling of having the most perfect day ever solidified.

Darkness fell. The baby went to bed. She locked herself in her bedroom, door closed. She had not been able to find wrapping paper, but there had been a huge roll of butcher's paper.

She had Christmas shopped a little for Jamey back in Calgary, so one-handed, she managed to get a chunky little train and some cars wrapped. Then she wrapped a few of his old toys, knowing full well he would not know the difference.

Now, what for Ty? She crept out of her room and retrieved his oven gloves. She cut her red toque, and a towel she had brought with her, and managed to patch the hole in the one. She wrapped it up. And then she went thought her suitcase, found the two books she had brought with her and wrapped those up for him.

Funny, humble little gifts.

That filled her with the Christmas spirit.

And when she came out, she had little brown paper wrapped packages, the wrapping lumpy and terrible, which she put under the tree with great and gleeful pride.

"Now," she told Ty, who was stretched out on the living-room sofa, nearly asleep, "I'm going to make us some hot chocolate. And then we can sing Christmas carols."

He snorted, but didn't say no.

Amy was in the kitchen, stirring a vat of hot chocolate when the phone rang.

"Hey, can you get that?" he called from the living room.

She picked it up, was thrilled with the caller and the invitation.

"That was Beth," Amy said, standing in the doorway. "She realized I was going to be here for Christmas Day. She invited us over for dinner. They have turkey."

"We were just there," he pointed out, something stubborn in the set of his jaw, a shield over his eyes.

"Surely you would have been joining them for Christmas dinner?" she asked.

He said nothing.

"You wouldn't go and be with your own father on Christmas Day? You'd rather sit here by yourself?"

Again he said nothing.

"I want to go. I have Christmas presents for them." She went and stood in front of him, folded her arms over her chest.

"How could you possibly have that?"

"I made them something. I already told her we would go."

"You shouldn't have done that. I'm not going there for Christmas."

"But—"

"I'm not arguing with you. And it's not open for discussion."

"Oh! Now you sound just like Edwin!"

She could tell he didn't like that one little bit.

"Look," he said, his tone cool. "We are not husband and wife. We are not even a couple. So we don't have to discuss decisions."

Regardless of the truth in that, Amy was not going to be the woman she had been with Edwin. Never again. Just deferring to him, trying to make him happy, avoiding confrontation, even when the price of that avoidance had been the loss of her own identity and her own soul.

"You're absolutely right. We don't have to discuss decisions. I'll go without you," she decided.

His mouth formed a grim line. "And how are you going to do that?"

"I'll take the little sled we used to toboggan with today. And I'll follow the track we made with the horses."

"With one hand?" he said with satisfied skepticism.

"That's all I need to pull Jamey on the sleigh," she said stubbornly.

His mouth fell open. "What happened to the girl who was afraid of her own shadow?"

Her eyes went to his lips.

He had happened to her. And she was a girl no more. She was a woman, and she was one who knew her own mind.

And this is what her own mind knew, standing there on Christmas Eve having her first fight with Ty Halliday.

The woman she had become was in love with him. Enough to believe, even given the stubborn cast of his features, that a Christmas miracle could still happen.

She went and sat beside him on the couch, covered his hand with her good one.

"Tell me what's wrong between you and your dad," she said, again.

She needed desperately to know that he felt he could trust her. She was aware that it was the only gift she wanted from him. And she wanted to give him the gift of not being so alone. That's what she had wanted to give him from the moment she had set up that tree for him.

And her hopes hung between them, in the silence, waiting for his answer.

# CHAPTER EIGHT

Ty felt her weight settle on the sofa beside him. He was surprised. He had used anger to keep people away from him for a long, long time.

Maybe he had used anger because it felt so much more powerful than what lurked right beneath the anger.

Sadness. A well of sadness so deep and so profound a man could drown in it, if he let himself.

But now Amy was beside him, and he felt that if he went down into that sadness, and it seemed like it would drown him, she would throw him the rope.

Crazy to think this little speck of a woman could save him.

Crazy to think he needed saving at all.

But he was suddenly so aware that he did. That he was alone and that he was lonely and that it was going to stay that way forever if he didn't take the risk of telling someone.

The old cowhands had a favorite expression that they had used liberally on him when he was growing up and made mistakes.

*If ya always do what ya always did, y'all always git what ya always got.*

And suddenly, Ty was aware of wanting something different. A new chance at his old life.

He was aware he was giving in to the temptation of wishing. He took a deep breath and hoped he wasn't going to be sorry.

"I told you already my mom left. I was a little older than Jamey, eighteen months or so. I don't remember it. My dad wouldn't say anything about it. Then or now. He didn't talk about her. It was pictures of his first wife, Ruth-Anne, who had died, in his wallet and on the mantel. Until I was four or five I thought the woman in the pictures must have been my mom.

"Then one day she phoned. My mother phoned. She said she wanted to take me to Disneyland but my dad wouldn't let me go.

"And then I never heard another word from her, ever. And my dad would just get this look on his face whenever I tried to bring it up. And believe me, I tried to bring it up. Because I had a mother! She was out there, somewhere. She wanted to take me to Disneyland.

"I was convinced she'd just show up one day. That I'd come home from school and come in the door and there she'd be. With a tray full of chocolate chip cookies. Or the Christmas tree up and decorated." He smiled a touch at that.

"My dad and I lived in this world that was pure guy. Horses and cattle, hard work and cowhands.

"But we were invited for dinner lots. And I'd see this other world. Where people had curtains on the windows, and there wasn't a tractor engine in pieces on the kitchen table, and a newborn calf on a blanket in front of the stove. They had nice dishes and their houses smelled like good things cooking, not motor oil and horses.

"And then I went to school. There's a thing called Mother's Day that I had been blissfully unaware of. Everybody makes a little plaster cast of their hand for Mom, or sticks macaroni on a plate with glue and paints it silver to make a wall hanging.

"Sometimes, if it was slow season on the ranch, I'd go home on the school bus with one of the other kids. Their handprints and macaroni art were hung on the wall. I stuck mine in a box I put it under my bed to give to my mom when she showed up.

"My friends' moms would fuss over me. Cut my hair if it was too long, mend my jeans, send me home with cookies.

"Christmas was the worst time to be a kid with no mom. Every other house looked the way this house looks tonight and never has before.

"Everybody had trees up, and socks hanging by the fire and stacks of presents. Kids talked about Santa. Sheesh! Santa? My dad told me that was a bunch of baloney when I was two.

"My dad's idea of a present? New leather work gloves. I got all the clothes I needed every year for Christmas—a pair of jeans, a couple of new shirts, and a new pair of boots.

"I don't want it to sound like I didn't appreciate it, but I wanted something else—a new book, or some music or a game. Something fun. Maybe even frivolous.

"In my mind, I was inventing a fantasy mother. She was a little bit of everybody's mom. Pretty like Mrs. Campbell, could make lemon meringue pie from scratch like Jody Wentworth's ma, she thought long and hard about just the right gifts, like Julia Farnstead. When I snitched my dad's whiskey, she'd ground me, like Mrs. Holmes, not make me clean stalls. And then after a couple of days of being grounded, she'd forget all about it, not have me up to my ass in crap for the next hundred years.

"I guess I was building kind of a head of steam against my dad even before it happened. We were butting heads. I was drinking and smoking and carousing, and he was pretty damn unhappy about it.

"Then, when I was seventeen, I came in one day, and he was at the kitchen table with his head in his hands, and this pack of letters in front of him.

"And he looked at me and said word had just got to him that my mother had passed.

"And he handed me these letters, said he had been waiting on the right time to give them to me, and it had just never seemed like it was it.

"I've never been so mad in my whole life. Killing mad. But he got up and left, and I took those letters and read them, and the fury just built.

"My mom loved me. She'd written me letters. And he'd never given them to me. Not a single one. Not even when he saw me pining away on Mother's Day, and on my birthday and at Christmas."

Ty thought he should stop then. His fury felt fresh and dangerous.

"Then what happened?" Amy's soft voice prodded him to go on.

"I packed my bags that night and left."

"At seventeen?" She was aghast.

"Quit school. Slept under a bridge the first couple of nights. Got hungry. But never hungry enough to come back. Finally, I found work on a ranch. I ended up riding a bit on the rodeo circuit.

"Wild years," he said with a shake of his head. "An angry young man taking out his anger on the world.

"And losing myself a little more every day. Taking stupid risks with broncs and bulls and life in general.

"Then I got a call my dad's been hurt bad in an accident. And I came home. We didn't really speak. He gave me the deed to the ranch, said it was mine now and he expected me to man up and look after it.

"And I did. End of story."

He waited now. For her to do the wrong thing. To prove to him his trust had been totally misplaced, that it had been a mistake to tell her.

He waited for her to give him some Pollyanna advice. To make him hate her by giving him sympathy.

But she did nothing at all. She sat there, and after a while she leaned her head against his chest.

And she whispered, "Oh, Ty. Oh, Ty."

Quite frankly, it made him feel as if he wanted to bawl his damned eyes out, which was what he'd been scared of all along.

But he put his hand to her hair and stroked it, and that sensation of fury disappeared, and so did the feeling he might lose control of his emotions.

Instead, a sweet sense of not being alone filled him.

She was absolutely silent, and yet he could sense her feeling for him. They stayed together like that in a wordless place of being utterly and beautifully joined, until his eyes felt heavy. He gave in to something. And he slept.

When he awoke, his heart felt tender. He carefully shifted out from under the weight of Amy's resting head, let her down gently on the sofa. Then he went to the back door and put on his jacket and went outside into the cold night air. It had stopped snowing, finally. He could see the great expanse of stars over his head.

He went to the barn and into the tack room, and got down the little saddle he had used as a small child. It seemed impossibly tiny now.

He wanted to give something to Jamey. And something to her. He didn't want them to wake up in the morning to no gifts from him, when clearly she'd been busy all day making sure everyone was getting something from her.

So in the cold of the tack room, under a bare light-bulb he worked long into the night cleaning and oiling the old, old saddle.

And when he was done, he went up to the house. Amy had got up off the sofa and gone to bed. It was past midnight—Christmas morning actually—and he was glad she had not waited up for him. He felt fragile. Some untouched part of him bruised.

He set the saddle aside and then took his most precious possession and wrapped it for her.

He put the saddle with a clumsy bow and the carefully wrapped copy of *Lonesome Dove* under the tree.

He realized he was giving away things that really mattered to him.

And that he didn't feel sad. Still, fragile, almost raw, but not sad.

He felt lighter than he had in years.

In the morning, she cried when she saw the saddle for Jamey. And cried even harder when she unwrapped the book.

He felt a little lump in his throat, too, when he found his oven mitts had been repaired. He squinted at the repair job. If he was not mistaken, the repair had been executed at the expense of her little red toque. And she had surrendered the two books she had brought with her to him. He hadn't read either of the authors before, but she promised him the books were not chick lit.

And then the real magic of Christmas happened. Jamey was put in front of a small pile of gifts, wrapped in butcher's paper.

He was thrilled that he was allowed to rip and tear. The contents of the first package spilled out—she had wrapped up his little wooden puzzle for him.

"Regifting," Ty said with a shake of his head.

"What would you know about regifting?" She laughed.

Jamey was way more interested in the paper anyway. He shredded it, and then moved on to his next package. A pair of Onesies fell out.

"Is that an elf suit?"

"I bought it before I came. Isn't it cute? He can wear it over to your dad's this afternoon."

Something in him froze. He'd told her everything. Surely, she didn't think he was going to go over there!

He'd trusted her. He'd thought she got it.

Now, looking at her, he wondered what he had expected. For her to choose a side? And for it to be his side?

*To be understood,* he realized. His expectation, his *wish* had been to be understood.

He had trusted her with his deepest hurt. He had told her about the man who had stolen Christmas mornings like this one from him. It was as if she hadn't heard a word, lost in her Pollyanna world. If she had heard what he was saying, she would know he didn't want to be around his father.

She was helping Jamey unwrap another parcel, taking a teddy bear from it, wagging it at him.

She didn't even know she had hurt him. Which was good. She never had to. It had stopped snowing. If he worked at it, today could be her last day here.

For a hallelujah moment it felt very flat.

"I'm going to go feed the horses and cows," he said. "Then I'm going to make a start on the driveway."

"It's Christmas!"

"I know." He deliberately turned his back on the magic that had very nearly caught him with its spell.

"I've got to check the turkey," Beth said.

It was a perfect Christmas moment: fire blazing in their hearth, Beth murmuring about the turkey, Hunter Halliday holding Jamey on the old wooden rocking horse he and Beth had given them.

It was the perfect Christmas, except for one thing: as soon as they had arrived, Ty had cast a glance toward the house, then headed for the machine shed. Moments later they had all heard a tractor start up.

"He's not coming in," Hunter said, casting her a glance. "You might as well relax."

"He'll come in for dinner, won't he?"

"I don't know. I doubt it."

"It's Christmas," she whispered. "I had hoped something would happen."

"Something did happen," Hunter said.

She liked him so much. She didn't know why he had kept those letters from Ty. But she also didn't know why Ty didn't just ask him. There had to be a reason. When she saw Hunter playing with Jamey she felt she could see who he really was.

And it was a man who loved deeply and completely, not someone intent on stealing his son's happiness.

Why couldn't Ty see that?

"You said something happened," she said to Hunter. "What?"

"You said he gave your baby his saddle."

"Yes, he did. I don't know why. It's not like I have a pony."

"Don't ever get a pony!" Hunter said. "Mean-spirited little rascals! Now, let me tell you about a gift like a saddle. It's not a saddle. It's a wish for your little boy. It's a hope that his future holds a good horse. Long rides. Camping under starry skies. The companionship of hard men who have your back. Someone to teach you to be a man."

Amy felt tears in her eyes. "You gave him that saddle once, didn't you?"

"And my daddy gave it to me."

"We can't take it then! It's a family heirloom."

"It's not about the saddle, Amy. It's about the wish. Ty hasn't made one of those for a very long time. So, maybe while you were waiting for one miracle, another came in the back door."

"Ty told me you didn't have any religion," she said.

"Don't need religion to see a miracle. Take me in this chair. I think I see some pity in your eyes."

She was embarrassed. "I just see the man you once were and know it has to be hard for you."

"Here's the thing—when I got hurt, Beth was my nurse in the hospital. Wouldn't have met her unless it happened.

"And here's the other thing—that boy of mine was killing himself on anger and self-pity and I didn't know how to bring him home.

"So, I could have my legs, but no Beth. And I could have my legs, but I would have put my son in the ground by now. So I can't walk. Maybe I didn't get the miracle I wanted, but I sure as hell got the one I needed. Lost my legs. Found my heart, got my boy back."

The tears that clouded Amy's eyes began to fall. She wiped at them.

"Don't go crying, now. Beth'll have my hide."

"Dinner's ready." Beth called. "Amy, will you tell Ty?"

She pulled on her boots and coat and followed the freshly plowed drive. He was a long way down it, and she waved her hands at him.

He turned off the tractor.

"Come eat. Beth has put a lot of work into dinner."

He looked as though he was going to refuse, but then didn't. She wanted the man he had been last night. So open to her. But he wasn't. He was remote and closed, and she wanted to weep at her loss. After a while, Amy wished he had stayed outside on the tractor.

He was ruining everything with his sour look and his terse way.

And right after dinner, he wanted to leave, even though Beth had the cards out and Amy thought it would make Christmas absolutely perfect to stay and play cards and laugh and get to know each other deep into the night.

The sleigh ride home didn't even seem magical. Jamey was crabby until he finally went to sleep.

"Your dad really cares about you," she finally said. "I think it's time to bury your hatchets."

"Yeah, in each other's skulls," he muttered.

"Stop it!"

He squinted ahead silently.

"Have you ever just asked him? Why would he do that? Why would he keep those letters from you?"

"Do you think any reason why would be good enough?" he asked quietly. "I've been watching you with your baby. I see what that relationship between a mother and a child is. If it was you and Jamey, could any reason someone kept him from you be enough?"

"You need to forgive him," she said softly, imploringly.

"Don't presume to know what I need. And you don't seem like any kind of expert on forgiveness yourself."

"That's not true," she said. "I have forgiven Edwin."

"Edwin?" he snorted. "It's not Edwin you haven't forgiven. It's yourself. You were so sold on your own fantasy world that you put the blinders on when it came to the man you picked. Because you wanted something so badly. That's what you can't forgive."

She felt stunned by how clearly he had seen her.

And by the truth of it.

And by the fact that making a mistake on Edwin had not killed that fantasy at all. Here she was, in love again!

Still willing to overlook glaring faults—his stubbornness, his hard heart—to have her fantasy. Of home. And family. And love.

"You know I could overlook a lot of faults, Ty, but you being mean to a cripple? That speaks to your character!"

"Yeah, well, if my dad ever heard you call him a cripple, you'd be off his Christmas list, too."

"You're missing the point."

"No. You're missing the point. Why would I care if you overlooked my faults or not? That would imply some kind of vision for the future. And I don't have one. Not with you."

That hurt! And she saw that he had intended for it to hurt. But as mad as it made her, he was absolutely right.

She had no business thinking about a future that included him. She had a lot of work to do. All of it on herself.

As they pulled up to his barn he glanced over.

"Well, would you look at that?"

She looked and saw a long line of headlights moving slowly up the driveway.

"Neighbors," he said. "Plowing me out."

"Does that mean I can leave?"

Why did he hesitate before he answered? "Yeah, you can leave."

"Good!"

She grabbed Jamey and, ignoring the pain in her

hand, leaped off the sled. She could not bear Ty touching her, helping her. She was going to be off the Halliday Creek Ranch before he even unhitched the horses.

## CHAPTER NINE

Ty knew as soon as he walked in the house that she was gone. He could feel the emptiness even before he saw all the things had been taken.

He had tried to drive her off with those last cruel words.

He went to his front window, and could see her little red car going down his freshly plowed driveway. He could see she had it so packed full of stuff that she couldn't even see out her back window.

Ty fought the desire to go after her, to follow her at a safe distance, to make sure she didn't get lost again, to make sure she made it safely to her destination.

But wouldn't it be better for all involved if she didn't know how much he cared? He didn't ever want her to come back here. Because how could you not pick up the gauntlet she had laid down? He would have to be a better man if he wanted a future with her.

And then he saw them.

He didn't know where they had come from. He thought he had stuffed those letters in his riding jacket pocket.

But there they were on the kitchen counter, the envelopes yellow, that blue ribbon tied around them.

He went and touched them. He told himself just to throw them out. That nothing could be gained by reading them again.

Except, he had been seventeen when he'd read them last.

And full of emotion. Anger. Bewilderment. The loss of something he had held on to and wished for his whole childhood.

He took the letters, tossed them on his dresser and went to bed. The first thing he thought of in the morning was Amy. The second was Jamey.

The third, before he was even out of bed, was the letters.

Suddenly, he knew he needed to read these letters now, not as a kid, but as a man.

He took them, went and made coffee, sat in his house that was too quiet and too empty, and pulled out the first letter.

An hour later, he set the last one down, squeezed the bridge of his nose hard between his thumb and his index finger.

When he was seventeen, he had read these letters and he had been as blind as Amy had been when she married her husband, he had wanted something so badly.

All he had seen was his mother's love for him and how his father had thwarted him. Now, older, wiser, he saw something completely different.

Every letter started with the same line.

*Hi, Ty. Are you missing me?*

And now he saw what he had not seen all those years ago. Not once did she say she was missing him. Not once. And that little blue ribbon held a dozen letters, which averaged out to less than one a year. The letters rambled on about things that would hold no interest to a child, *her* shopping trips, *her* travels, *her* concerns with weight, and hairdos and gym routines and boyfriends.

As an adult, Ty saw things he had overlooked when he'd first read them. He saw a certain sly undermining of his father: claims she wrote lots of letters and that his father probably withheld them. That she sent cards and gifts for his birthday or Christmas, but she was sure his father could not be trusted to pass them on.

How could he have missed this when he first read those letters?

And then he realized, he hadn't. At some level he had recognized the truth staring straight at him.

He'd been abandoned. And she didn't care about him. Not even a little bit.

And at seventeen, he hadn't been able to handle what that had opened up inside of him. So much easier to be angry at his father. So much more powerful a feeling than to face the sadness of it all. To face the real ending of his wish. If he could convince himself that she was the one who had been wronged, then she could still be the good person he had imagined.

He remembered, as a kid, hearing the word *amnesia* for the first time. That such a condition existed had made him ecstatic. It would explain everything. And excuse everything.

Now, having reread the letters, Ty saw the truth. His mother had walked out. She hadn't cared about the child she had had. She had not thought about him, or wondered about him, or dreamed of coming to tuck him in or make him cookies. She had not had amnesia. His father had played only the smallest role in her abandonment of her child.

At seventeen, he had not been able to face that reality. Amy was right.

Kind, gentle, sweet Amy was right.

He needed to ask his dad the one simple question. Why? And he realized why it had been so hard to do that. Because part of him had known it had nothing to do with his dad. He was pretty sure he knew the answer, but he had to ask it anyway. It was time to man up.

He was glad his road was clear and he could drive to the old homestead place. It felt as if taking the sleigh there would pull what was left of his heart right out of his chest. All he would think of was her, and her awe of the experience, and that little baby with them.

When he arrived, he knocked on the door and his father told him to come in. He was obviously alone. Of course, it was the first day in several that the roads had been open. Beth was no doubt taking advantage of it to restock the household.

His father looked eagerly over his shoulder. "Where are Amy and Jamey?"

"Gone. The roads opened. And I doubt if she'll be back. She was good and mad when she left."

His father nodded. "Karma's a bitch," he said.

"Amy didn't think I'd given you a fair shake. She said all I had to do was ask."

"So you're only here because Amy thinks you should be?"

"No. I'm here because I think I should be."

His dad nodded, satisfied.

"Why?" Ty asked softly. "Why didn't you give those

letters to me? I read them again. I think I know the answer, but it's time to hear your side of it. I should have asked a long time ago."

Ty tossed the letters down in front of his father. He watched as his father picked them up with worn hands, turned them over, something resigned in his face, but strong, too, ready to weather the storm.

"Were there more of these?" Ty asked.

"No. I tied up everything that came with a ribbon to give to you. Someday."

"Were there cards and gifts? For my birthday? For Christmas?"

"No, son. There weren't. Not ever."

It was as he had suspected when he'd read the letters; a lie contrived to cast a bad light on his father. Or maybe to convince a child—not that hard to do—that she was not the negligent one.

He dropped into the chair across from his father. "I need you to tell me."

His dad glanced at him, and something flickered in his eyes. Ty was ashamed that he was able to recognize it as hope.

"Tell me about my mother," he said softly.

And his father sighed and glanced at him again, then nodded. "All right. But maybe I need to tell you about me first. I'm just a simple man, Ty. Hardly been off this ranch, don't have a whole lot in the tool kit to help me handle things that are complicated. I think you figured out I'm not really a man of letters. School was hard for me."

"Yeah, I figured that out," Ty said.

"I was married before your mama, you know that."

"For the longest time I thought Ruth-Anne was my mother," he said. "That's whose picture you had on the mantel and in your wallet."

He was taken now with the look on his father's face, an almost dreamy look at the mention of Ruth-Anne.

"We were sweethearts from middle school. We got married right out of high school. I was only eighteen. You know that never should have worked, but damn, it did. We thought we were going to have us a pile of kids, but for whatever reason, she couldn't. I suspect now it was a warning that something was wrong, but that warning took twenty-five years to play out.

"Aw, Ty, twenty-five of the best years. Working together. Playing together. Filling all those spaces where the kids would have been with each other."

Ty was staring at his father, trying not to let his jaw drop.

"She died of cancer after we'd been married twenty-five years. I can't even tell you about that kind of pain, so bad it was a mercy when she finally went. And then my world opened up to a whole new kind of pain. I didn't know what to do with it. She'd been my earth. Everything.

"So I drank and lived hard and reckless and on the very edge, hoping the man upstairs would get the message and take me, too.

"But he dint. Nope. Those years are a blur of bad living, like attending a never-ending party in hell. I hooked up with your mama. Oh, boy. I'd met a woman who could match my hard living and raise me some. Her name was Millicent, though she never went by anything but Millie.

"And then, just like that, the party was over. She told me she was pregnant."

He cast Ty a long sideways, measuring look.

"I want to know it all," Ty said, reading reluctance in his father's expression.

His father nodded, as if deciding something. "She said she'd decided to get an abortion. She said she'd had an abortion before. That it was no big deal."

His father's hands were clenching and unclenching unconsciously. "No big deal?" he whispered. "Me and Ruth-Anne would have done anything to have a baby. And now I was going to throw one away? It just went against my grain. Nothing in the way I was raised prepared me for a notion like that.

"I knew, that second, the party was over. The self-pity was over. I had a job to do, and I'd better step up to the plate and do it. I convinced Millie to marry me and have the baby.

"We moved back out here to the ranch. It had been neglected for quite some time. I nearly lost the place, and I was aware I could still lose it if I didn't knuckle down. The work was unending. You know what it's like now. It was ten times worse then. Trying to build a herd, every fence and building falling down. I wasn't young anymore, I was in my mid-forties by then."

His voice drifted away for a moment. "I'd been partying in hell before, now I was just in hell. No party. Your mama, she couldn't stand this place. She was lonely and restless and bored. She wouldn't come work with me, like Ruth-Anne had always done, so she'd sit in the house. She didn't cook a meal or clean a floor. She

just watched her soaps on TV and brooded on things
to fight about.

"By the time I'd drag my sorry ass through the door
after putting in a fourteen or fifteen-hour day, she'd be
ready. That woman could fight about anything. If I said
it looked like rain, she'd say snow, and the war was on.

"I thought it was my fault. Working too hard, not
paying enough attention to her. I thought it might be
because she was pregnant and hated everything about
that state. She didn't see herself as growing the most
beautiful thing on earth. She saw herself as fat and ugly.
And I'm ashamed to say I got tired of trying to convince
her otherwise.

"She started accusing me of having a girlfriend
on the side. I'd walk in, so tired and wet and dirty I
could barely keep my feet, and she'd come and sniff my
neck. Claim she could smell a woman on me. And I'm
ashamed to say, I got tired of that pretty damn quick,
too.

"And then you came along. God almighty, Ty, I ain't
saying this just because you were mine, but you were
the most beautiful baby ever born. Golden hair, like a
little lion, and bright eyes, and this lusty voice. Powerful
for a baby. I just stood in amazement of you from the
first second."

Again, the hesitation, the sideways look. But Ty had
read the letters. He had already guessed this part.

"Tell me," he said.

"Aw, Ty, it's what I never wanted to tell you. You've
seen cows who reject their calves? Basically, she was
indifferent to you. She was aghast at the idea of breast-
feeding. That was for *animals*.

"I'd come in from a hard day, and it was more of the same. She thought I'd been seeing someone. And she'd start screaming it was my turn to look after the baby, my turn to change diapers and feed you.

"As if it was a burden," his father said, soft, still shocked by it. "It was no burden. Hell, Ty, you were what I lived for. Those moments when I came in and picked you up and saw after what you needed. And then I'd take you and plant you right in the middle of my chest, and we'd both fall fast asleep on that sofa.

"After Ruth-Anne died, I'd pretty much given up on love. And Millie had soured me even more. But when you and I would fall asleep on that couch, I believed in love again.

"I came home one day early, and one of the ranch hands was coming out of the house. He wouldn't look me in the face, muttered something about Millie calling him about the plumbing.

"I was so fed up, I was beyond caring what she did. I can see now that just added to the problems. The more I didn't care, the more she tried to make me care. She thought she could make me jealous, but all it did was make me worry she might be neglecting you.

"So I got myself one of those kangaroo pouch things and popped you in it. My saddle bags were filled with diapers and formula. You literally were on a horse before you could walk. If I had a real hard day lined up, I'd drop you off with one of the neighbor ladies.

"One day we came home and she was gone. She'd smashed every single dish in the house and every picture frame, she'd cut up all my clothes, but she was gone.

"And I didn't feel nothing but relief.

"I tried to be a good dad, but when I think about it, I probably wasn't. I wasn't much of a talker. And I was strict as all get-out, like that would make it seem like I knew what I was doing when I didn't. Scared to let you know how much I loved you, like it might turn you into a sissy boy or something.

"I knew you longed for a mama. Anytime we went to a neighbor's you were scouting out a female to attach yourself to. And I figured that was enough. I mean, our friends and our neighbors circled the wagons around me and especially around you. You were raised by every woman in this whole community, which is probably why you turned out half-decent.

"It was four years before I heard from her. Just phones up one day as if she suddenly remembered she had a little boy. Told me her and her new husband wanted to pick you up and take you to Disneyland.

"Like I said at the beginning. I was just a simple man. I didn't know what to do with a complicated situation. But I didn't really trust your mama. Once she had you, what if she just disappeared with you? And I sure as hell wasn't sending you to Disneyland with a man I'd never met.

"So, I told her no, and then she asked to talk to you. I knew how bad you wanted a mama, so against my better judgment I put you on the phone. When you got off, you were looking daggers at me and screaming that you wanted to go to Disneyland with your mama.

"You wanted a mama so badly, and now one had magically appeared. But all I could see was trouble and broken hearts, so after that when she phoned I'd say you were at a neighbor's or something. It wasn't often.

Once or twice a year, then not for several years in a row. Same with the writing. A letter here and there once she figured out you were old enough to read, I guess. I opened the first few of her letters, and I knew nothing had changed. It was all about her. Suddenly, you were old enough that she could try and use you to fill up that horrible hole inside of her.

"And right or wrong, I wasn't having it. I told myself when you were old enough to sort it out for yourself, I'd tell you about it. But somehow the time never seemed right, because you always seemed so hungry for a mama that I knew you would never see her for what she was.

"I tried to protect you. And I doubt I did it right, and yet if I had the same choice to make again, I would make the same one. So how can I even say I'm sorry?"

"Why didn't you just tell me? Dad, all these years. Lost."

"They weren't lost, son. You had a chance to step out of my shadow, to become the man I always knew you would be. Every father and son goes through it. I did with my own daddy and had no excuse for it, either."

It hurt him that his father had held faith in him through all these years of stubborn distance. He felt tears pricking at the back of his eyes.

"And the last few years gave me something, too," his father said. "All those years, you were my first responsibility. Love had banged me up pretty good. Then when I got hurt, I was alone, and Beth was alone, and—" He shrugged. "Beth tells me now, your mama was probably sick. Bi-Polaroid."

"Bipolar," Ty said softly. It made sense. It fit with

what he had read in the letters, the manic pages of writing, followed by months, even years of silence.

"The way I see it I had Ruth-Anne. And she was
earth. And I had Millie and she was fire. Beth was and
is like a cool drink of water on a hot day."

"Did you ever wonder if I was yours?" Ty asked
softly. "I mean, it sounds as if she might have played
it hard and fast."

His father looked genuinely shocked. "Of course not!
You're way too stubborn to be anyone else's. Besides,
you are now, and always have been, my sky, so bright
it nearly hurts my eyes to look at you.

"Once I had a narrow view on life and wouldn't have
put stock in such things, but now I see I've had a life of
perfect balance, earth and fire, water and sky.

"I don't have any regrets, Ty. Your mother brought
me you. This chair brought you back to where you be-
long."

"All these years," Ty said. He knew now it wasn't
his father he'd had to forgive at all. It was his mother.

And in some part of him, he had probably known
that all along.

"You go after that girl who was here. You go after
her and that little boy. They both need you. If you don't
mind my saying so, it's time to grow up, Ty. You ain't
a little boy pining after your mama anymore. There's
nothing like someone needing you to make a man grow
up."

"I don't even know if she'd have me, Dad. She'd re-
sent the implication that she needed me."

"Now you're talking nonsense. To their great detri-
ment, women just love us Halliday men. They'll put up

with quite a bit from us. See what we could be, see the diamond underneath all that coal, and get damned determined to mine it. She needs you, all right. And you need her."

Amy looked out the window of the McFinley house. It was a nice house, custom-built on a small acreage some twenty miles from the Halliday Creek Ranch. The views were not as sweeping as the ones from Ty's front window—she could see the neighbors' place—and it lacked the charm of the homestead.

It was a typical January day in southern Alberta—bright blue skies and teeth-numbing cold.

"A good day to bake bread," she told herself out loud, as if that could ward off the loneliness. Jamey was napping. Terrible to wish he would wake up so that the huge emptiness inside her could be filled with his laughter and gurgles, his energy and motion.

Perhaps she was imagining it, but he, too, seemed subdued.

One of the things he had got for Christmas, when they had made it to Cynthia's, was a farm set, with buildings and horses and cows.

Jamey had a favorite horse. He called it Ben. And when he played with it, he mournfully and softly called Papa Odam over and over again.

So she knew she would not bake bread. The memories of the last time she had baked bread, Ty laughing beside her, putting his muscle into the kneading, were just too intense.

For a while, she acknowledged, being snowed in with

Ty, having Christmas at the homestead place, she had touched what she had always wanted.

It had filled her to overflowing. It had been better than the dream.

Now, despite this beautiful home, despite her internet business taking off and filling most of her waking hours, she could not outrun the feeling. The feeling of loss.

She had spent six days on the Halliday Creek Ranch.

She felt as if she was mourning it more profoundly than the loss of her husband. Of course, that dream had already been shattered.

Her time at the ranch had breathed hope into her when she had convinced herself all hope was gone.

And now, gazing out the window at the icy beauty of the landscape, she felt as though all hope was gone again.

Somehow, she thought he would have called.

As deeply in the thrall of all those good memories as she was.

And somehow, she was not sure how, she had found the courage and pride not to call him. Especially as she read *Lonesome Dove,* savoring every word, feeling some connection to Ty as she read it.

But no, it was time for her to make it on her own. Time for her to stand on her own two legs. Time for her to forgive herself all her mistakes by drawing power from who she was now, what she could accomplish, her considerable strengths and talents.

"So, cookies it is," Amy said, forcing herself to move from the window. "Chocolate chip."

The doorbell rang as she was taking the last of them from the oven.

She went and opened it. The most adorable teenage girl she had ever seen stood there. She was about thirteen, owlish behind glasses. She had an armful of books, and flashed a shy smile that revealed braces.

"Mrs. Mitchell?"

"Yes?"

"I'm Jasmine Nelville. Ty Halliday sent me to babysit. He said to tell you I have my babysitting certificate, and that I can give you references. I've been babysitting for two years."

Amy looked at her visitor, stunned. She noticed a car in the driveway, and realized it was Jasmine's mother, who waved and drove away.

"Right now?" she stammered.

"I think he's right behind us. Of course, he's hauling, so that takes longer."

"Hauling?"

"Is that the baby?" Jasmine said when a wail filled the house.

"Jamey. He's just waking up from his nap."

Jasmine brushed by her, set down her books and followed the sound. With Amy trailing dazedly behind her, she went into the bedroom and picked Jamey out of his crib.

"Oh!" she said blissfully. "What a handsome boy."

Jamey preened.

"Mrs. Mitchell, you need to get ready. Dress warm. And he said to tell you to wear sensible boots."

"But—" She heard clanking and thumping and a big, diesel engine. She went to her front window and watched as Ty jumped out of the cab of his truck, went and opened the back door of the trailer he was pulling.

One horse, saddled, backed out. And then Ben, also saddled.

The rational part of her knew that she should say no to this. He hadn't even called. He didn't even know if she wanted to go with him.

But the rational part of her could hardly be heard above the singing of her heart. It was not time to be rational. She had been rational all her life. Even when she had chosen Edwin, it had been a rational decision based on what she wanted, and on what he seemed to be.

Stable. Safe. From a good family. Able to provide.

That was what she needed to forgive. The great injustice she had done Edwin when she had chosen him for what he was, instead of who he was.

And that man outside, calmly tightening cinches, waiting for her?

She knew exactly who he was. Exactly. She ran for her coat and her boots and raced out the door.

He looked up and saw her coming, smiled at her over the top of the saddle, and then came around the horse and opened his arms.

She flew into them. And he lifted her high and swung her around, and then set her down and gazed at her like a man who had crossed the desert and she was his drink.

"What are you doing here?" she asked, breathless.

"Why, Miss Amy, isn't it obvious?"

"Not really."

"I've come a-courting."

"Oh!" she said, suddenly shy.

"You're an old-fashioned girl in a new-fangled world. So with your permission, I'm going to do this in an old-fashioned way. I'm going to wine you, and dine you and bring you flowers. I'm going to sweep you right off your feet."

Was there any point telling him he already had? No. Why miss the fun?

He helped her onto the horse. He told her it was an old mare named Patsy and he called her dead-broke.

But it didn't matter. She would have felt no fear being put on a fire-snorting, head-tossing, feet-dancing stallion right now.

They rode out the McFinleys' driveway and down a snowy road. He rode right beside her, asking her about Jamey and the house and Baby Bytes.

And she asked him about Beth and his dad, and as they rode, he told her all of it. About reading the letters and reconciling with his father.

"Been working hard at being the man you'll expect me to be," he said.

The skies were so bright, and the air so crisp. They rode for nearly an hour and then he found a way down to a frozen river, and set a picnic blanket out in the snow. From his saddle bags, he removed hot chocolate and sandwiches on bread that was flat and might have tasted quite terrible if he had not mentioned he had made it himself.

He took out a book of poetry and read to her. He looked up at her, mischief winking in his sapphire eyes.

"It's on the first-year university reading list," he admitted. "Do you know what it means?"

"Not a clue," she said.

And then the sound she lived for bubbled up between them, louder than the water running under the frozen blanket on the river.

Their laughter. And then somehow, they were rolling around on that blanket, and he was on top of her, pushing her hair back from her face and covering her with kisses. Her ears, her lips, her neck, her eyelids.

Homecoming.

An hour later, they were heading for home, nearly frozen on the outside, a fire so deep burning on the inside that Amy felt as if she would never be cold again.

And so the courtship began.

Ty amazed her with his deeply romantic nature. True to his word, he wined and dined her at some of the finest restaurants in Calgary. He brought her flowers. They went to movies and for long walks and horseback rides.

He began to include her in community activities. He brought her to fund-raisers and dances and pancake breakfasts where she met his neighbors and his friends. He brought her out to Beth and his dad's. They did things with Jamey—the indoor swimming pool, sleigh riding, quiet evenings at home playing on the floor with his toys and reading him stories.

The seasons were changing, winter giving way to the tender promise of spring, when Ty invited her to his place, asking her to drop off Jamey with his dad and Beth.

When she arrived, the two horses were saddled in the yard.

She mounted hers with confidence, a brand-new bravery in her.

That's what love had given her. The bravest of hearts. The most tender of hopes.

They followed a winding trail along Halliday Creek and then up and up and up the mountain.

Finally, they broke from the woods and crossed alpine meadows on fire with wildflowers, still going up.

The horses picked their way through rocks, and then Ty stopped and offered her his hand as she dismounted.

Hands intertwined, they climbed up yet some more, scrambling over rocks, his hand helping her, pulling her.

And finally they stood at the very crest.

Amy could barely breathe. She was standing on top of the world. She could see everything for a hundred miles. Ty's house and the old homestead were like dollhouses far down in the valley. Contented cattle grazed on new grass.

And he stood beside her, strong and sure. The strongest man she had ever met.

Only, when she pulled her eyes from the panorama of the view, that strong man was on one knee before her.

He had a ring box in his hand and was gazing up at her with a look in his eyes that dimmed the panorama of what she had just seen.

"Amy," he said softly, "you know I am not a religious man. But even so, I thank God as I know Him every single day for that wrong turn you took in the road.

"I thank Him for bringing me your smile and your laughter and your ability to listen and your ability to see things in me that I had never seen in myself.

"I thank Him for bringing your son into my world and for allowing me to know what it is to be a dad to that little boy."

To her amazement, the strongest man she had ever known suddenly looked shy.

And maybe even a little scared.

His gaze drifted from her to the view. "Do you remember when I read *The Iliad?*" he asked.

"Yes."

"Achilles had to choose between *nostos,* homecoming or *kleos,* glory. If I had that choice to make? I would choose homecoming. I would choose coming home to you.

"I cannot imagine my world without you. Amy Mitchell, I am asking if you would consider being my wife?"

She took his chin in her hand and drew his gaze back to her. In the sapphire of his eyes she saw her whole world and the future beyond.

She saw laughing babies and cattle and horses, she saw books and movies and heated discussions and quiet moments.

She saw what she had yearned for her entire life.

In the quiet strength in his eyes, she saw a place where neither of them ever had to be alone again.

She saw home.

She whispered yes, and he leaped to his feet and gathered her in his arms and then he lifted her and swung her around and shouted "yes" over and over and over again.

And his affirmation of love and of life, his shouted yes, reverberated off the mountains and the valleys, and echoed back to them and surrounded them.

In glory.

"Some of us don't have to make a choice at all," Amy told the man she loved. "Some of us are allowed homecoming and glory."

## EPILOGUE

Ty came out of the barn, leading the pony. It was saddled—that same saddle that he had given Jamey all those years ago. The pony had a red plaid Christmas ribbon woven into his mane and was tossing his head because of the red bow attached to his thick forelock.

His father disliked ponies, and had argued that for Christmas they should give Jamey a horse, just as he had given Ty a horse when he turned five.

But Ty had liked this pony. It had a soft eye and a willing way, and it was pretty with its lush black mane and the big brown spots all over it.

He sniffed the air as he moved toward the homestead place. Snow. It was going to snow very soon.

He hoped not too much.

A man, he thought wryly, should be careful what he wished for.

Because, really, he did not want to get snowed in right now.

The old homestead place had been his and Amy's for just over a year. After Amy and Ty's twin girls, Millie and Becky, had been born, his dad and Beth had suggested the trade. The new house was more practical for the older Hallidays, with its one floor and two bedrooms. It had been easy to make it one hundred per cent wheelchair accessible.

And the old homestead place had the four bedrooms upstairs that had been closed up for years.

Amy had taken that on as if she was on an episode of *Save This Old House.* The old homestead house was refurbished to shining. Every nook and cranny had her stamp on it, her love sewn into drapes and cushions and pot holders…and little pink baby blankets.

Now, on Christmas Eve, it was filled to the rafters. Her parents were here. And Jamey's grandparents.

For a long time, Ty hadn't known quite how to forgive his mother for her abandonment and indifference. But then, at Amy's suggestion, they had found out every single thing they could about her.

And they had discovered he had a grandmother, and an aunt and uncle, and a passel of cousins.

His grandmother, Elizabeth, had been shocked that she had a grandson. Since her daughter had been in her teens she had disappeared for long lengths of time and would eventually resurface with no explanation about where she'd been.

Elizabeth was desperate to meet Ty. When they had first met, she had kept touching his face and weeping. They had connected almost instantly, and through stories and pictures and shared letters, unraveled the mystery of his mother.

If the mystery of mental illness could ever really be solved.

Millicent Williams had always bounced between two extremes. On one side, his grandmother told him, her beautiful daughter had been high energy, on fire, talk-

ative, charming, brilliant, sensitive, creative, passion-
ate, charismatic. On the other side she had been needy,
manipulative, darkly sensual, secretive, jealous, selfish,
conniving, and capable of unbelievable cruelty in her
ability to use people and discard them.

Ty had learned his mother had suffered a disease of
extreme self-centeredness where everything and everybody in the world were perceived only through the
filter of how they could benefit her.

And because of that, she alienated everyone she had
ever touched, had ended up alone, increasingly desperate, highly dependent on the alcohol and prescription
drugs that had led to her demise.

It was a tragic tale of undiagnosed illness.

When Ty looked at pictures of her, he felt a strange
and gentle tenderness for the woman he had never
known. He knew that he looked at his own life differ-
ently because of her.

Jamey, as far as he could tell, came from generations
of solid, pragmatic ambitious people. But as he watched
his own girls, the twins, just turning one, he sometimes found himself wondering how early you would
see signs of it.

His father had told him, even though he had never
defined it as mental illness, he had watched him the
same way.

Nowadays, at least, there was more chance of it being
caught. Treated. Not ignored or mislabeled.

His mother had just been considered wild. And unpredictable. Untamable. A lot of people had given up on
her way before his dad entered the picture.

When he thought of her now, he felt his heart soften

with sympathy. There was no anger left for the woman who had abandoned him with hardly a look back. He felt he loved her, despite it all.

And maybe that's what forgiveness finally was.

The ability to see it all in a larger way.

The lights from the windows of his house poured out over the snow, golden and warm. He could smell the wreath on the door. Amy had insisted on Christmas lights, and the whole place was lit up in traditional red and green. It had taken him about three weeks to get all those lights up tracing the lines of the roof, and every time he'd wanted to just forget it, he'd look down at Amy, tumbling around in the snow beneath him with the twins and Jamey, their happiness echoing on the air.

So hanging a few Christmas lights was a small price to pay.

The front door opened, and the noise from inside spilled out. Laughter, conversation. His family.

And wasn't it what he had always wanted?

*Be careful what you wish for,* he told himself again wryly. He and Amy would sleep on a mattress on the floor of the back porch tonight, snuggled together to keep warm because they had given up their bed to Amy's parents, Dolores and Adam, who were recovering from jet lag.

Cynthia and John had the guest room. Before she was done, Cynthia would refold every single towel in the house and arrange the tinned goods in order of their size, labels to the front. She would tut disapprovingly over baby clothes put in drawers without being pressed.

Amy's parents would bring out flowcharts and trap him into a discussion about a business plan for the ranch, and all their great ideas to make Baby Bytes the most visited website on the planet. They didn't understand that Ty was working at nights online to get a university degree for the simple love of learning, not so that he could turn the ranch into the most viable business enterprise ever.

Cynthia, John, Dolores, Adam, none of them got the concept of *enough*. That you could have enough and be enough. That you could quit trying so hard and just enjoy the plentiful gifts life had given you.

He saw Amy standing on the porch, hugging herself, watching his approach.

She was rounder than she had been, her curves full and womanly. Her hair had inexplicably lost its curl after the twins were born, and it hung in a soft, lush wave to her shoulder.

But her eyes remained the same, and the curve of her mouth.

A long time ago, without knowing, he had ridden through the dark to a light she had put on, without knowing it was for him.

At the beginning of all of this, he would have said that he and Amy were about as different as two people could be. She was city. He was country. She was small. He was big. He was rugged. She was refined. She knew all about computers and cell phones, and he used technology only reluctantly, as a means to an end. He liked nothing better than a good book. She liked nothing better than a good movie.

But underneath all those superficial differences, Ty knew he and Amy had the most important things in common.

They had both wished for that place called home.

And at one time, they had both given up on that wish.

It almost seemed the universe was offended by this refusal of its greatest gift, the refusal to love.

It almost seemed as if the universe had conspired to bring them together, had put Amy on the wrong road, that led them both to the right place. The only place.

She flew down off the steps and snugged under his arm, petting the pony.

"Hello, Sampson," she crooned to their newest family member.

One small, perfect moment, just the two of them, and then the door flew open and Jamey came flying down the steps, screaming the word Ty never ever got tired of hearing.

"Papa!"

Behind him, Cynthia appeared, one of the twins, Becky, in her arms, freshly washed and a new bow in her hair. "A pony? What are you thinking? Jamey is just a baby! Surely, he'll be killed."

And Amy's mother, Dolores, had the other baby, Millie, who was clinging to her early gift of a Baby Einstein calculator.

Dolores nodded her agreement with Cynthia, and added, "I can't imagine what it costs to feed one of those for ten years or so."

Ty didn't even bother telling her a pony, if you were lucky, could live for thirty-five years.

John and Amy's father spilled out onto the porch, too, arguing about stock prices, not even aware there was a pony in the yard. Or three grandchildren nearby.

His father wheeled out and scowled across the yard

at them. "A pony! Sheesh. I told you to get a horse. I've never met a pony I liked."

*Be careful what you wish for,* Ty told himself, remembering that long-ago wish to be part of a family.

He showed Jamey how to use the stirrup, refused to help him, even when his grandmother Elizabeth called out, "Ty, lift him up, for Pete's sake. It's too hard for him to get on by himself."

Beth called from in the house, "I've nearly got dinner ready. Don't be out there too long. Jamey doesn't have a coat on!"

Yes, be careful what you wish for.

Jamey, with a hoot of pure satisfaction, managed to heave himself into the saddle. Ty passed him the reins.

"You are not going to let him ride by himself!" Cynthia cried.

But he was going to let him ride by himself. As he watched the boy who was the son of his heart, Amy, who had once been afraid of everything, breathed her fearlessness after Jamey. She snuggled deeper under Ty's arm and sighed her contentment.

The pony stopped partway across the yard and Jamey flailed away, to no avail, trying to get the pony moving with his heels.

"I told you," Hunter said grumpily, "you should have got him a real horse."

The smile pulled harder on Ty's mouth.

He had wished for this thing called family.

And he would not change a thing.

\* \* \* \* \*

# REQUEST YOUR FREE BOOKS!
## 2 FREE NOVELS PLUS 2 FREE GIFTS!

### Harlequin
## Romance

#### From the Heart, For the Heart

---

**YES!** Please send me 2 FREE Harlequin® Romance novels and my 2 FREE gifts (gifts are worth about $10). After receiving them, if I don't wish to receive any more books, I can return the shipping statement marked "cancel". If I don't cancel, I will receive 6 brand-new novels every month and be billed just $4.09 per book in the U.S. or $4.49 per book in Canada. That's a savings of at least 14% off the cover price! It's quite a bargain! Shipping and handling is just 50¢ per book in the U.S. and 75¢ per book in Canada.* I understand that accepting the 2 free books and gifts places me under no obligation to buy anything. I can always return a shipment and cancel at any time. Even if I never buy another book, the two free books and gifts are mine to keep forever.

116/316 HDN FESE

Name _____ (PLEASE PRINT) _____

Address _____ Apt. # _____

City _____ State/Prov. _____ Zip/Postal Code _____

Signature (if under 18, a parent or guardian must sign) _____

Mail to the **Reader Service:**
**IN U.S.A.:** P.O. Box 1867, Buffalo, NY 14240-1867
**IN CANADA:** P.O. Box 609, Fort Erie, Ontario L2A 5X3

Not valid for current subscribers to Harlequin Romance books.

**Are you a subscriber to Harlequin Romance books
and want to receive the larger-print edition?
Call 1-800-873-8635 or visit www.ReaderService.com.**

\* Terms and prices subject to change without notice. Prices do not include applicable taxes. Sales tax applicable in N.Y. Canadian residents will be charged applicable taxes. Offer not valid in Quebec. This offer is limited to one order per household. All orders subject to credit approval. Credit or debit balances in a customer's account(s) may be offset by any other outstanding balance owed by or to the customer. Please allow 4 to 6 weeks for delivery. Offer available while quantities last.

**Your Privacy**—The Reader Service is committed to protecting your privacy. Our Privacy Policy is available online at www.ReaderService.com or upon request from the Reader Service.

We make a portion of our mailing list available to reputable third parties that offer products we believe may interest you. If you prefer that we not exchange your name with third parties, or if you wish to clarify or modify your communication preferences, please visit us at www.ReaderService.com/consumerschoice or write to us at Reader Service Preference Service, P.O. Box 9062, Buffalo, NY 14269. Include your complete name and address.

HR11B

*Is the Santina-Jackson royal fairy-tale engagement
too good to be true?*

*Read on for a sneak peek of
PLAYING THE ROYAL GAME by USA TODAY
bestselling author Carol Marinelli.*

* * *

"I HAVE also spoken to my parents."

"They've heard?"

"They were the ones who alerted me!" Alex said. "W
have aides who monitor the press and the news constantly.
Did she not understand he had been up all night dealin
with this? "I am waiting for the palace to ring—to see hov
we will respond."

She couldn't think, her head was spinning in so man
directions and Alex's presence wasn't exactly calming—
not just his tension, not just the impossible situation, bu
the sight of him in her kitchen, the memory of his kiss. Tha
alone would have kept her thoughts occupied for days o
end, but to have to deal with all this, too…. And now th
doorbell was ringing. He followed her as she went to hit th
display button.

"It's my dad." She was actually a bit relieved to see him
"He'll know what to do, how to handle—"

"I thought you hated scandal," Alex interrupted.

"We'll just say—"

"I don't think you understand." Again he interrupte
her and there was no trace of the man she had met yes
terday; instead she faced not the man but the might o

rown Prince Alessandro Santina. "There is no question
at you will go through with this."

"You can't force me." She gave a nervous laugh. "We
oth know that yesterday was a mistake." She could hear
e doorbell ringing. She went to press the intercom but his
and halted her, caught her by the wrist. She shot him the
me look she had yesterday, the one that should warn him
vay, except this morning it did not work.

"You agreed to this, Allegra, the money is sitting in your
ccount." He looked down at the paper. "Of course, we
uld tell the truth…" He gave a dismissive shrug. "I'm
re they have photos of later."

"It was just a kiss…."

"An expensive kiss," Alex said. "I wonder what the
apers would make of it if they found out I bought your
rvices yesterday."

"You wouldn't." She could see it now, could see the
orrific headlines—she, Allegra, in the spotlight, but for
ameful reasons.

"Oh, Allegra," he said softly but without endearment.
Absolutely I would. It's far too late to change your mind."

\* \* \*

ick up PLAYING THE ROYAL GAME by Carol Marinelli
on November 13, 2012, from Harlequin® Presents®.